THE SIGNPOST UP AHEAD

<u>Short Story Collection</u>

Portals of the Mind

<u>Individual Short Stories and Novellas</u>

Another Stupid Time Travel Trip

Electronic Telepathy

Ode de la Lune

The Barn

The Melting Man

The Poem

<u>Screenplays</u>

Batman DarKnight (with Lee Shapiro)

Paradigm (with Eric Kaplan)

Maelstrom

THE SIGNPOST UP AHEAD

A SHORT STORY COLLECTION

STEPHEN WISE

ARROWHEAD
PUBLICATIONS

HUMAN
AUTHORED
AG Authors Guild
7032057

For Kenny

You introduced me to the fantastical world of The Twilight Zone and the absurdity of Monty Python, for which I am eternally grateful.

Imagination...its limits are only those of the mind
itself.

— ROD SERLING

CONTENTS

Preface   xi

Electronic Telepathy   1
It's Logical   35
Ode de la Lune   39
Derelict   55
The Chosen One   61
Bananas   67
Mom   71
A Perfect Copy   77
The Poem   87
Closing Time   95
The Bully   103
Just a Phase   109
Sweat Equity   115
The Barn   123
Viking Funeral   133

Afterword   145
About the Author   149
Arrowhead Publications   151

Common wisdom says an author should focus on one genre to become a brand, and creating a continuing series will ensure longevity of your career. Essentially, repeat yourself ad nauseam.

I'm not good at listening to such advice. I write what strikes my imagination, which throws my stories into a wide range of genres and styles. I love science fiction, horror, fantasy, murder mysteries, suspense thrillers, and adventures, to name a few. My own writing, whether in screenplay format or prose, reflects this. While I would love to assemble a collection that focuses on a single genre (and maybe I will at some point), this publication bounces all over the place. Expect the unexpected, as the cliché goes.

This is my second collection following *Portals of the Mind,* and what lies on these pages is a variety of genres, but also some of the most personal stories I've ever written. I've culled events and details from my life, but twisted them around to not be biographical. Those close to me may still recognize certain aspects taken from reality, but the goal is to entertain and hopefully shed some light on the human condition.

Join me as we go on an adventure with these fifteen short stories that will introduce you to an android sleuth, a creature that lives in a barn, a misunderstood prophecy, a conductor hiding his beastly nature, a killer copy machine, a severe penalty for staying in a store after hours, and more. These were fun to write, and some were cathartic. I hope you get as much out of reading them as I did writing them.

—Stephen Wise, February 4, 2024

Electronic Telepathy

O fficer KL-124, or Kal to his teammates, received the transmission of a 187—homicide. As it was 2:43 A.M., he was on his sleep cycle with all but the automated systems on standby mode and his power port plugged in to recharge his batteries. Normally, he ran two to three weeks without recharging, but he had been feeling sluggish, and a quick check revealed the energy cell was down to thirty-five percent.

Kal emerged from his sparse quarters, which provided a modicum of privacy that was more for his human co-workers than for himself, and entered the forensics lab. Motion sensors triggered the overhead lights to illuminate, though he could see in the dark just fine. Except for special occasions, the human police officers in this unit worked a traditional eight to five schedule and left after-hours investigations to Kal, which was his function, after all.

In the parking garage below the station, Kal chose the sedan that belonged to the Cybernetic Forensics Investigation Unit. As soon as he closed the door behind him, he connected to the vehicle's CPU through his wireless Electronic Telepathy and started the silent electric engine. An instantaneous data transfer told the car its destination, and it rolled out onto the deserted street.

Kal usually drove manually instead of of using the car's self-driving mode. It was his way to have dominance over what he considered lesser machinery, and the tactile feel of his hands on the wheel and control on the road satisfied him in a manner he did not quite understand. However, his response time lagged, so he turned the driving over to the more primitive A.I. under the hood. This lag would be imperceptible to humans, but Kal noticed it. Though this wasn't enough to cause concern, he planned to perform a full diagnostic of his hardware and software as soon as he had a free moment.

The city is beautiful this time of night, Kal thought. It was a marked difference between the bustle and chaos of daytime streets. Lights stretched up the sides of towering buildings, brightening the sky with multiple colors. During the day, the sky was gloomy with little sunlight breaking through the peaks of the skyscrapers; but at night, it was like a canvas illuminated with neon paint.

The route to the crime scene brought Kal through the seedier side of his precinct, where most of his cases transpired. In this part of the city, the night was alive with humanity who rarely saw the sun. They filled their lives with drugs, illicit sex, and violence. Many previously outlawed vices were legalized in recent years. However, it didn't change the situation these poor creatures lived in day to day, and it didn't quell the turmoil that infiltrated the streets. Not for the first time, Kal wondered how a species that seemed intent on killing itself could create such magnificent pieces of art and technology—himself included.

Not everyone, he corrected himself. Some people were kind at heart and wanted to lead good lives. But even the best of them struggled with problems, both internal and external. Kal considered the possibility there was a flaw in their programming, in this case DNA, that prevented humans from ever reaching full potential, both as individuals and as a population.

I don't have perfect programming, either. Of course, imperfect humans created me, so there's no way they could produce perfection.

High-rise buildings gave way to blocky warehouses and industrial parks. Old-fashioned ground rails spider-webbed the open expanses between behemoths that lay like monstrous carcasses under the yellow gloom of ancient sodium-vapor lamps. Chains of boxcars stood on the rusty tracks like sleeping serpents. Concrete suspension railways for high-speed trains criss-crossed overhead, a more efficient means to transport goods to ever-demanding consumers.

Kal approached a modern building incongruent with the dilapidated structures surrounding it. A sign out front marked it as being the state headquarters for the Interstate Transit Bureau. Red and blue flashes showed police activity. He commanded the car to park behind one of two patrol cruisers near the main entrance. A third vehicle, a standard-issue unmarked city police four-door, denoted a detective.

If I were human, I could rise to the rank of detective. I should consider myself fortunate to be designated an "officer." The lab analyzer doesn't have that honor.

Kal exited the car and strode to the patrol officer posted at the door. The officer glowered at him, his lips curling back in an inadvertent scowl. Kal was used to such reactions. Though he was modeled after a human male with an unobtrusive medium build and an unassuming five-foot-ten height, he could not hide the artificiality of his appearance. He was aware of the term "uncanny valley" that referred to human-looking objects that created unease and even revulsion in the onlooker, though he was uncertain why he would cause that reaction despite seeing it almost daily.

"I am Officer KL-124 from C.F.I.U.," Kal said to the patrol officer. He held up the badge that hung around his neck as emphasis. He wore a white uniform that all members of his team were issued, rather than standard police blues, and sometimes other cops found it hard to believe he was on the force. "I was directed to report here and assist in the investigation."

"Detective Sokolvich is inside." The patrolman spat the words, as if trying to dispel an unpleasant taste from his mouth. "Down the hall to the end, second door on the left."

Kal followed the directions, though he would have located the crime scene based on the activity. A second officer stood next to a man sporting graying stubble and wearing a security uniform. Kal assessed that the security guard found the victim and reported it to the police. The detective on the scene had already questioned the guard, who was now standing by in case further questions arose. Upon seeing Kal, the guard's mouth dropped open and his pupils dilated, a reaction Kal associated with unease in humans. To his credit, however, the patrol officer remained dispassionate and waved Kal through another doorway, which led to an anteroom of a larger office filled with cubicles.

The victim lay dead on the floor, face-down in a pool of blood soaking into his expensive suit. Two more patrol officers stood nearby while Detective Sokolvich, a man in his fifties who could stand to lose thirty or forty pounds, snapped photos of the scene. He glanced up at Kal with bloodshot eyes.

"I am Officer KL—"

"Yeah, fine. I was expecting you." He raised the device in his hand. "I know you'll record the entire crime scene, but I want my own evidence. Sometimes human brains can work better than artificial ones."

Kal wanted to tell Sokolvich he had nothing to explain, but remained silent. The detective displayed an aggressive temperament, so Kal took care to not escalate hostility. He had a job to do, regardless of Sokolvich's feelings toward him.

"Have you identified the victim?"

"Waiting for you to do it, Artie." The nickname "Artie" was a derogatory term often given to beings with artificial intelligence. "The force paid a lot of money for you, so we might as well get our money's worth."

He knows I'm artificial. Why does he think insults will hurt my feelings? Kal turned his attention back to his job. "Any relevant information I should know before starting my sweep?"

"The guard never saw the vic before. The room was locked and alarm armed."

"Would the three of you please step into the hall?"

Sokolvich cocked his head toward the door and the patrol officers exited the room. It was standard procedure to allow the C.F.I.U. team full access to the crime scene, and the other cops should not have even been in this room until Kal arrived to conduct his forensic analysis. In his experience, police who worked overnight tended to be sloppy and often contaminated crime scenes. Sokolvich remained in the doorway, a minor act of defiance that told Kal *he* was still in charge.

Kal scanned the body, first with a regular vision, then with ultra-violet, infrared, and several other filters that picked up traces unable to be seen by human eyes. He would record organic residue such as hair, bodily fluids, and even fingerprints left on clothing and would gather all but the most microscopic of any biological samples he detected.

He searched all pockets for identification, but found no wallet, and then rotated the corpse onto its back, taking care not to smear any more blood. Upon locating a bloody hole in the front of the victim's suit, Kal inspected closer and discovered a bullet hole in the left side of the man's chest. No exit wound existed. Using the size of the wound, the body's position, and the dimensions of the office, he calculated the calibre and trajectory of the bullet. He used the limited X-ray technology built into his vision and detected a metallic mass embedded in the victim's damaged heart.

Excellent shot, but in these conditions, the killer didn't need to be an expert marksman.

Kal recorded an image of the victim's face. The man died with his eyes open, which would help with facial recognition. He connected to his vehicle's network via Electronic Telepathy and searched the police database for matches. The results were ninety-eight point three percent accurate that this was State Senator James Boggins. To confirm, Kal placed his fingertips onto those of the dead man, whose open hand was still pliable, being only in the early stages of rigor mortis. The sensors on his fingertips recorded the man's fingerprints, and they matched the senator's.

He continued to evaluate the deceased, retrieving fibers from his clothing, samples from under his fingernails, and even scrapings from his teeth, to analyze further at the lab. Based on evidence, the approximate time of death was three hours ago.

The floor revealed no clues. A lot of footprints, as expected in a business office. Based on residual heat signatures, the most recent sets belonged to the police. Beyond that were the prints of the victim himself. No sign of a second person in the room at the same time Senator Boggins was killed.

Kal followed the victim's tracks. He entered through the door that Detective Sokolvich was blocking.

"Excuse me," Kal said. "I need to examine the hallway."

Sokolvich huffed, then stepped aside to allow Kal to continue his investigation.

"Boggins had approached from the main entry," Kal explained to Sokolvich. "He stood outside this door momentarily, presumably to disarm the alarm, then entered the anteroom. Within several minutes—I am unable to determine the exact time—Boggins was shot and died from blood loss. The killer did a good job covering his tracks, literally."

"What was he doing here at midnight in the first place?" Sokolvich asked.

"Unclear."

"Did he have any connections to the Transit Bureau?"

"One moment." Kal accessed the database again. He found no police records, so broadened the search to news reports and official government filings.

"Damn, that's creepy," one of the patrol officers said under his breath. Of course, Kal heard it. When he ran network searches, his body fell even more into the uncanny valley, and it was often unsettling to onlookers. He hoped his manufacturers, Eden Labs, developed an upgrade soon to prevent this reaction—even a blinking light that would show activity instead of just stiffening like a mannequin with blank eyes.

The search ended within seconds. "Senator Boggins served on the committee that oversees guidelines in how the state interacts with the Interstate Transit Bureau, which is under federal jurisdiction. Each state has authorization to legislate how best the I.T.B. operates within its borders."

"Riveting," Sokolvich said. "It brings us back to why he was here, and who he was with. A politician doesn't just show up at a federal installation in the middle of the night for no reason."

Kal turned to the security guard. "I need access to the main alarm console and security camera recordings."

The guard escorted Kal and Sokolvich to a back room with a console filled with monitors showing various angles of both inside the building and the property outside. He shifted from one foot to the other, keeping as much distance from Kal as possible.

"You saw nothing on these screens?" Kal asked.

"I-I wasn't in here during the time of…I would've been outside doing my rounds. Here, I'll show you."

He typed on the keyboard and then the main monitor switched to a view of the rear of the building with a timestamp of 11:35 P.M. The guard appeared on the screen, meandering along the grounds.

Sokolvich checked his notes for the guard's name. "Arliss, right?"

Arliss, the guard, nodded.

"How long does it take you to do your rounds outside?"

"Maybe a half an hour."

"And you saw nothing out of the ordinary?"

"Not until I found…you know…"

"No one else you know of on property? You didn't see any cars?"

"N-no, sir."

"Okay. Pull up the video of the room where the murder took place."

Arliss typed again, and then frowned. "I don't understand. The recording for that camera is gone."

Sokolvich turned to Kal, as if expecting some answer from him. Kal raised his eyebrows.

"Try the hallway."

"Not here, either." Arliss ran a hand over his mouth. He typed again. "And I just tried cameras in the parking lot and front entrance. Nothing."

"Erased or never recorded?" Sokolvich asked.

Arliss shrugged. "Doesn't make much of a difference."

"Where is the access panel for the security system?" Kal asked? Arliss flipped open a hinged cover to reveal several data ports. Kal retrieved a cable from a hidden slot in his wrist and plugged it into a port. He accessed the data with an emergency police override code. "The videos were not erased. Those cameras were turned off at 2047."

"That wasn't me," Arliss said in a panic. "My shift didn't start until ten. I can prove it."

Sokolvich sighed. "No one is accusing you. We're just trying to gather the facts."

"It wasn't done from this console," Kal said. "I located a breach. Someone tied in remotely."

"How? This is a closed system."

"It is equipped with an emergency back door for the security company and federal agencies."

Sokolvich rubbed his temple. "That means anyone could have hacked in."

Kal nodded, a gesture he picked up from his coworkers. "I want to check one more thing." His body stiffened again as he conducted another search. "The alarm pads to the main entrance and to the crime scene show no activity once they were activated at 1730, not even when you arrived, Detective. My assessment is whoever deactivated the cameras also turned off the recording function on those pads."

"Premeditated murder," Sokolvich said. He put his hand behind his head and stretched.

THE SENATOR'S BODY WAS TAKEN TO THE MORGUE, WHERE IT would remain in stasis until the investigation was complete, upon which time the police would release it to next of kin for proper disposal.

Detective Sokolvich retreated to his own office to file the report, grumbling about the mess this murder was causing—a case this high profile would involve the highest level of the police department, the media, and government officials, all of whom would apply pressure to solve the crime with urgency. Kal sympathized with him because he knew the detective was in over his head. Sokolvich worked the overnight shift for a reason—it was none of Kal's business, but those hours were reserved for rookies, those with behavior problems, or old-timers who were marking time before retirement. Sokolvich was no rookie, so Kal could only speculate on which of the remaining categories fit the detective.

Kal returned to the lab with the evidence he gathered, both physical and virtual. He ran analysis on the samples from the crime scene, but nothing brought him any closer to finding the identity of the killer. Since the physical evidence did not lead anywhere, he turned his attention to the virtual.

He recalled the coding of the security system he stored

in his memory and examined it line by line. The hack entry point was obvious, but the hackers left no breadcrumbs to lead back to them.

They must have made a mistake somewhere. Humans always do.

He repeated the procedure hundreds of times, searching for something he may have overlooked. He was closing in on a thousand when his teammates reported to work, so he paused the search to greet them.

Officer Raul Ortega arrived first, as usual. He had spiky blue hair that went against department regulations that was overlooked because he was on a special crime unit. He liked an outrageous appearance, but his work ethic was impeccable.

"Hey, Kal! You're up early. Got an overnighter, huh?"

"Yes. I'm still working through my analysis."

"With dedication like that, you'll make detective any day now."

Kal frowned at Ortega's obvious untruth, but processed it as an attempt at ironic humor.

Sergeant Maria Fontana burst in with Officer Jennine Yoshida right at her heels. Fontana wasted no time with pleasantries and directed her attention to Kal. "I saw Sokolvich's report. What's your take?"

"Guess we're diving in headfirst this morning," Ortega said. "Fully clothed. No goggles."

Fontana shot him an icy glare, and he shut his mouth.

Kal recited what he learned from the investigation so far. Fontana kept constant eye contact with him. *She could pass for an artificial being herself.*

Ortega leaned forward and propped his elbows on the corner of the desk to listen to the recount.

Yoshida busied herself with morning activities. She had never quite warmed up to Kal, though she tolerated him. Despite her feigning disinterest in his report, her tilted head gave away the fact that she was indeed paying attention.

"Let's go over what we know and what we don't," Fontana said. This was Detective Sokolvich's case, but it was the responsibility of the C.F.I.U. team to deliver to him whatever evidence they could decipher, so he could make an educated call. They often solved the cases, leaving the lead detective to make the arrest. "At 8:47 P.M., someone unknown hacked into the security system of the Interstate Transit Bureau and deactivated specific cameras and alarm pads. The security guard arrived on duty at ten, and at 11:30 started his rounds outside. During this time, Senator Boggins and our killer entered the building, sight unseen. They went into that office where Boggins was shot and killed. The perp departed, leaving no evidence of his having been there."

"Or her," Ortega said. "No need to assume it was a man."

Fontana pursed her mouth at him. "The *killer* left no evidence. Including any residual heat signature. Two hours later, Haverback discovered the body. Our unknowns: why Boggins was there; who he was with; how the killer left no trace; and how the security system was hacked."

"How did the killer get away?" This was the first time Yoshida spoke since arriving. "Just vanish into the night?"

"The senator's car," Kal said. "It was not at the I.T.B. building."

Fontana turned to Yoshida. "Run a check on the registration of any vehicles Boggins owned, then trace their GPS locations throughout the night."

Yoshida sat at a workstation and concentrated on the computer.

To Ortega, Fontana said, "Find out everything about the Transit Bureau oversight committee Boggins was on. I want to know his position on it, anything controversial, opponents he may have had, whether he had any financial interest in it. Everything."

It would be more efficient if I conducted that research, Kal thought. *I can process information exponentially faster than they can. But maybe I overlooked something that requires a human brain to register, some connection that would pass right by me because I don't have the proper context. I can deliver facts, but not nuance.* Kal watched as Ortega and Yoshida worked. They were serious, dedicated, and skilled. *If I had those human qualities, they would become obsolete. I wouldn't want that.*

Fontana addressed him. "I need you to continue working on the hack. We *have* to get to the bottom of it. Examine it from all angles. Try to reverse engineer it if you have to. What would *you* do if you needed to hack into this?"

"I will do my best." *What if my best isn't enough? This is possibly the most important case I ever worked on. What if I fail? Maybe it would prove that artificial intelligence is too limited, that containing it in an android body is too expensive? They would transfer my intelligence into a computer, and there*

I would remain, forever unable to be independent. A virtual slave.

"Kal?"

He snapped back to the present.

"I thought I lost you there for a second. Is everything all right?"

"Yes. Later I need to run a diagnostic. I've detected some abnormalities that need to be addressed. Nothing serious, I assure you."

"Okay. Get to work."

HOW WOULD I HACK IN? KAL RAN A MYRIAD OF SIMULATIONS in attempting to breach the security system, but the architects did an excellent job at installing barriers. He concluded that the only way for someone to access it would be to already know the programming or to use a government override.

How about police emergency access codes? They worked for commercial-grade systems, but would they be successful on a federal facility? He had his doubts.

Kal used thousands of configurations that were all blocked—and then one worked. He tried it repeatedly, and each time he gained entry. He examined the code from the inside. The hack had the same digital footprint as the login of the access pad at the crime scene the previous evening.

This means the hacker is a police officer. Or at least someone with access to police technology.

Kal opened his mouth to tell Fontana his discovery when she said, "Press conference."

The sergeant activated the broadcast monitor, which showed the police station's briefing room. Several officials, including the Police Chief herself, a striking woman with silver hair, stood behind an empty podium with Detective Sokolvich at her side.

"Where'd they scrape up that roadkill?" Ortega asked.

"That's Detective Sokolvich, the lead detective on the case," Fontana said. "He used to be a damn fine cop. Rumor has it he found his wife in bed with another man. An altercation happened, and they nearly booted him from the force. By the grace of God, he kept his badge, but he sunk into the bottle and vanished to the graveyard shift."

"Broken hearts make broken men," Ortega said, throwing Yoshida a significant glance.

Yoshida scowled at him. Kal noted that her body temperature increased by half a degree and the capillaries in her cheeks swelled, allowing a rush of blood to discolor her flesh.

On screen, a well-coiffed man with a deep tan wearing an expensive suit stepped to the podium. Kal recognized him as Mayor Boudree. *If I didn't know he was human, I would think he was artificial.*

"I have the displeasure to announce a tragic circumstance," the mayor said into the microphone. "Last night, State Senator James Boggins died in an apparent homicide. We have notified his wife and family members, as well as the governor. With more details of the investigation, here is Chief Thomason."

Boudree stepped aside to let the Police Chief take the mic. "Thank you, Mayor Boudree. The murder happened last night at the main offices of the Interstate Transit Bureau. Officials are cooperating with the police department. Until further notice, that office is closed. We will update you when we have further information to share."

With that, Chief Thomason and Mayor Boudree departed. Detective Sokolvich and the other members of their entourage followed as the press corp shouted questions.

The broadcast changed to a news anchor regurgitating what had just happened moments ago. The on-screen image changed to video of the then-living senator with his arm around an attractive blonde woman in her forties. "Senator Boggins was married to cybernetics engineer Kristen Ashby of Cascade Robotics."

"Kal, that's your mom," Ortega said.

"I was designed and manufactured at Eden Labs," Kal said. "Cascade Robotics makes components."

"We've gotta get moving," Fontana said. "What do you have for me?"

Yoshida said, "One of Boggins's cars was out gallivanting around last night. Looks like he drove randomly for a couple hours before ending up at the I.T.B. building at 11:32 P.M. Sure enough, it left there at 11:54 and made a bee-line across town to a shopping center, where it now sits. The senator's phone geolocation records correspond to the vehicle's movements until it reached the I.T.B."

"Get a patrol to secure the car. You and Kal go out there and turn it upside down."

Kal accompanied Yoshida to the parking garage, though she ignored his presence until they got to the unit's sedan. "I'm driving. I like to have my hands on the wheel."

"Me too."

Yoshida gave Kal a quizzical look. "What's the difference between you or the car driving?"

"I'm either the driver or a passenger."

"Regardless, I don't want a computer making decisions for my life."

"Ninety percent of traffic is automated. Aren't you letting those computers make decisions for your life?"

"My reaction time is in my control. I'll be responsible for whether I live or die in a car."

"When I'm your passenger, you'll be responsible for whether I live or die as well."

"Except you're not alive." She shook her head and climbed into the car. "I'm arguing with a coffee pot."

Kal sat down in the passenger seat and fastened his seat belt. "I'm not a coffee pot. However, I'm sure I can learn to make coffee if you so desire. I won't promise how good it'll taste."

Despite herself, Yoshida laughed.

KAL AND YOSHIDA EXAMINED EVERY INCH OF BOGGINS'S car inside and out and found nothing out of the ordinary.

Kal collected a handful of samples from the seats and floor. While he lifted various fingerprints that were days —if not weeks—old from the passenger door, the only prints found on the steering wheel and driver's door belonged to the senator. The vehicle's CPU provided no leads as to another driver.

"Are we dealing with an imaginary killer?" Frustration creeped into Yoshida's voice.

They waited until Impound came to collect the car before heading back to the police station.

As Yoshida drove, Kal said. "May I ask you something personal?"

Yoshida's hands gripped the steering wheel tighter and her jaw clenched. "What?"

"You had a romantic relationship with Officer Ortega, correct?"

"So?"

"Earlier he made a comment about broken hearts making broken men. You had a physical response—"

"Is there a point to this?"

"I didn't mean to offend. I'm just trying to understand interpersonal relationships better to help me improve my job."

"Your *function* is to collect and analyze evidence. That's it. Not to psychoanalyze humans. That's beyond your capabilities."

"I apologize. I've made you upset."

Yoshida turned to him as if to continue scolding him, but something in his demeanor caused her to return her attention to the road.

When they returned to the lab, Ortega said, "Gather 'round, children. It's story time."

Fontana joined the three of them at his desk.

"It seems the good senator was not only supportive of high-speed rail coming into the state, he was a vocal proponent of it. With good reason—he owned stock in multiple companies that contributed to building and operating the rail."

"So he profited off it," Fontana said. "How would that relate to his murder?"

"Let's just say that several other unsavory organizations competed for control over it."

"I thought it was federally run," Yoshida said.

"Federally *authorized*," Ortega said. "But you know how those anti-big government politicians love privatizing everything? Boggins helped push through legislation. It seems the companies that want to get their grubby hands on it are *family* run."

"You think this was a mob hit?" Yoshida asked.

Ortega threw his hands in the air in a show of innocence. "Just presenting the facts. But there's another wrinkle to this sordid affair. Zoning. It's no secret that when the government claims eminent domain to build transportation access-ways, they tend to—correction, they *always*—do it in the poor neighborhoods. They don't care who they displace as long as it's not those with money or power. When they brought the high-speed rail into the city, they made enemies with some groups that fought back." He listed several organizations that conducted legal representation for minority and underrepresented groups, and concluded with a militant one tied to violence.

"This doesn't connect," Fontana said. "Why not take out a hit on him? Why bring him to the I.T.B. office and go through the trouble of hacking into their security and stealing his car afterward?"

Ortega shrugged.

"Keep working. Maybe something will break. Ortega, look into every potential connection to organized crime. If they're involved, they'll leave bread crumbs. Yoshida, I want you to investigate any community activist groups that may have a grudge against Boggins or the I.T.B. Let's get some solid theories going. I want to package what we know by end of business and send it to Sokolvich. Let him put the pieces together."

Kal kept the information about the use of a police code to hack into the I.T.B. security system to himself for now. He wanted to have a clearer understanding before reporting it.

He set about analyzing the samples he collected from Boggins's car. Of course, he found the senator's own DNA, but he also found hair samples and fingerprints that matched his wife, Kristen Ashby, which made sense. He also found fibers from his or Yoshida's uniforms, which sometimes happened.

Another sample belonged to a different person. The computer took longer to find a match because the owner was young with a lack of bio-data on file, but was identified as Jasmine Holman, one of Boggins's aides. It made sense that she would have ridden in his vehicle at some point, and since neither hers nor Ashby's bio-data were recent enough to conclude they had been in the car last night, neither were probable candidates for being the mystery driver, and hence the killer. However, Kal noted that both needed to be included in the report for Sokolvich to do any necessary follow-ups.

He moved on to visual evidence. Cameras blanketed the city, so it was likely he would find video of Boggins's car, especially now that he had its accurate geolocation from last night. He plugged in the data and started with police drone footage. Automated drones that remained airborne for up to four hours patrolled the city. Similar to what Kal had found at I.T.B.—every single drone along the route of Boggins's car was missing footage that night. He was now certain this was an inside job—that someone within the police department tampered with the evidence. Upon a thorough analysis into the programming, he learned he was right, except he could not trace the vandalization to its source.

Kal then searched for other governmental and privately owned security cameras connected to the network. Many of those, in particular the private cameras, required overrides with special permissions or even a bench warrant to access. If he broke into their systems and found something to help his case, it would be inadmissible in court and he could face penalties for violating the law. He knew a "gray area" tactic the police used—break the rules to learn the truth and then gather evidence through proper channels to make the case legally. It surprised Kal his programming allowed him to even consider it.

He hit roadblocks at every turn. He located exactly one video that captured Boggins's car driving down the road, but it was at such a distance and angle where it was impossible to see who was inside it. On a whim, he tried one other approach—social media. He searched through thousands of posts across multiple platforms and then found a match. At 2202, a man in his twenties posted a video of himself and his girlfriend on a date in a park downtown. Behind them, the image revealed Baggins's car parked on the side of the road. A hooded figure, possibly male of medium height and build, walked up to the car and entered the passenger side. The interior light came on, revealing Boggins behind the wheel. The passenger's face was obscured.

Kal searched other photos and video on social media taken during that time in the same location. He found one of several young people throwing a glow-in-the-dark frisbee. In the background, the same hooded male exited a sedan, but both the subject and the vehicle were too distant from the camera to be well-defined.

One more search, this time between 2200 and midnight. It seems the subject left his own car near the park to ride with Boggins. Kal was not lucky enough to locate footage of the subject returning to his car, but he found a shot of the parked vehicle itself—it bore a strong resemblance to the one owned by the Cybernetic Forensics Investigation Unit, the very one Kal had driven a couple hours later to the crime scene.

"That can't be," he said. He realized he had spoken aloud and looked around to see if any of his co-workers had overheard him. They were all focused on their individual work.

It couldn't be one of them. Could it? None of them are the right size. Possibly someone else within the department borrowed the car and returned it before I was called into action.

The subject must have returned to the car, but if he used a taxi or personal driver service, records could be located. Kal looked up the bus schedule and found a route that had one stop near the shopping center and another a few blocks from the park. He broke into bus's security camera—at this point he didn't care if he was breaking the rules. He would deal with that later.

At 2328, the subject boarded the bus. His hood covered his face. He rode that way until the bus arrived at his stop, when he stood up. For one frame, his face was exposed.

Kal stared at his own image.

No, no, no, no, no. That can't be possible.

His internal temperature rose. While his circulatory system differed from humans, it still performed functions for his body, and the pressure increased as the pump analogous to a heart became erratic. His vision blotted as his processor tried to make sense of what he saw.

Get control of yourself. You won't be any good if you let your circuits melt down.

Kal played back all his memories of the past twenty-four hours. He worked in the lab until after the rest of the team departed for the day. At 1830, he shifted into sleep mode to recharge his battery, then awoke at 0243 hours when he was called for duty.

Is it possible I did this while in sleep mode? While his programming didn't outright prevent him from doing harm to a human—otherwise certain aspects of his job as a police officer could be compromised—an action like this was out of character for him. And what would be the motive?

Fontana looked up as Kal approached her. He said, "I need to run my system analysis now. I'm experiencing some unusual activity."

She dismissed him, and he retreated to his private quarters. He connected himself to the machines and engaged the analysis. From his perspective, time passed instantaneously, but in reality, he had been disabled for almost an hour. He wondered if this was how humans experienced sleep.

The evidence was there—someone had tampered with his programming and wiped his memory last night. He discovered two other instances of that occuring over the last three weeks. Prior to the first wipe, a code was implanted into his operating system that was gibberish to him, and he would have to analyze it later to see if he could crack it. However, he was confident this code allowed the unknown intruder into his mind to seize control of his body. Further scrutiny revealed instances where the intrusive code replicated and modified itself, adapting to whatever situations it was running across. This was highly developed engineering.

Kal fought the urge to slam his fists into the console despite not being coded for violence—in fact, he was gentle. He was an investigatory tool, nothing more, designed to be the least threatening of humans as possible. His stature, demeanor, and even strength and agility were intended for intellectual work, not physical prowess.

However, his A.I. was also programmed to learn so he could adjust to new situations and interact with people more naturally. He was unfamiliar with this sensation. It was unpleasant, but he wanted to feed it like stoking a fire that burned inside him.

He was used as a murder weapon. Who pulled the trigger?

Someone had to have access to his CPU, invading his very essence. He felt betrayed, violated.

I want to hurt someone. As soon as the thought popped into his head, he deleted it. He did not hurt. He did not kill. Yet, he did.

The first suspects were his co-workers, who had direct access to him—they were all intelligent and trained for criminal data investigation. However, Kal did not believe any of them possessed the necessary skills. One of them might be an accomplice, though what would be the motive to sabotage their most advanced piece of technology? Fontana respected him, Ortega treated him as one of the team, and even Yoshida acknowledged his importance to solving crime. He doubted one of them would do this, but humans had proven to be unreliable in their expected behavior. Until he knew how the intruder gained access to his system, he could not trust the C.F.I.U. team. This disappointed him, but it was the best course of action.

How will they react when they find out I was the murder weapon? Send me back to Eden Labs as defective? Return my CPU to factory settings, wiping all my memories and everything that makes me who I am? Or will they be able to clean the infection from my programming and allow me to continue on the job?

Another unfamiliar sensation crept in, and it startled him to realize what it was.

I'm scared.

Kal pushed that away. He had a job to do. Regardless of how unsavory, the discovery was a breakthrough in the case.

I could hide this. No one would ever know.

No, he couldn't do that. He would complete his mission, no matter where it led. First, he had to gather the evidence to make a solid case.

He emerged from his chamber to find the lab empty. Lunch time. That made things easier.

Kal went to the parking garage and linked with the sedan via Electronic Telepathy. As expected, last night's GPS records had been deleted.

I sure was busy.

Kal contemplated several pieces of this puzzle. What gun did he use? Ballistics would reveal the type of gun, so if it was police-issue, that would point to an inside job. If not, where did he get it? He assumed he disposed of it—and the clothes he wore to conduct the murder—before returning to the lab. *I'd be very efficient, so those items would never be found.*

It was logical to conclude that Kal himself broke into the security system at I.T.B. and also used police codes to erase the video from the city's security drones and other cameras on his route last night.

Why go to the I.T.B. office to commit the murder? A reason must exist. And more importantly, Senator Boggins drove around town before meeting me as if he was losing someone tailing him and then willingly brought me to that office. He couldn't have expected me to murder him, but he still didn't want it known he was meeting me.

Then another thought occurred to Kal: *Why didn't I delete the GPS tracking from his car? The only reason is so information could be found.*

It all began to click. The killer wanted the motive to appear connected to the Interstate Transit Bureau—but what if it wasn't?

Kal still had several puzzle pieces to fit into place and suspected one would be found at the lab. Sure enough, he discovered Senator Boggins's wallet in a locked evidence box. He needed more research to determine if his suspicion was correct, but he would do that remotely.

One thing was certain—the person behind this was cold, calculating, and efficient. Much like a computer. Kal appreciated that.

KAL WAITED UNDERNEATH A CEMENT SUPPORT FOR THE high-speed rail high above. This property was once farmland on the outskirts of the city limits, unlike in the inner city where blocks of low-income housing had been razed to make room for the behemoth. Any cameras here would point at the rail itself for maintenance and safety reasons—the ground below was an electronic wasteland.

A luxury sedan veered down the rutted dirt road that bisected this section of the track. The setting sun glinted off the windshield.

I wonder if it's in self-driving mode.

It parked next to the C.F.I.U. sedan.

An attractive woman in her forties with long blonde hair stepped out of the car.

Kal had been uncertain if she would show up, but apparently his text compelled her:

> The code didn't erase all of last night's memories. I need you to do it manually and wipe it clean, otherwise they may use it as evidence against you.

The woman suggested this location because of its remoteness and lack of recording devices, and Kal suspected it was the same place they met for her to give him the gun.

Kristen Ashby, Senator Boggins's wife, regarded Kal through dark sunglasses. She may have needed them for driving toward the setting sun, but if she thought they would disguise her appearance, she was mistaken. She removed a case from the back seat, set in on the trunk, and then opened it. Inside was a variety of component and electronic tools.

"Okay, let's get to it," she said with no preamble.

Kal stepped toward her. "I disposed of the gun and clothing."

"I have no doubt."

"I haven't had a chance to plant your husband's wallet in Jasmine Homan's vehicle. That will be done tonight when I go into sleep mode."

"That's fine. You made sure his blood is on it?"

"Yes."

"Good."

"My memory is glitchy. Most of last night is missing, but random images pop in. Meeting Senator Boggins in the park. Going into the Interstate Transit Bureau office. Pulling the trigger. Seeing his blood spill out onto the floor."

Her mouth tightened into a thin line. "I don't want to hear about it."

"The look of shock on his face. He wasn't expecting it. There was so much blood."

"Enough."

Is she bothered because her husband died such a violent death, or just by the gruesome details of it?

Kal allowed her to plug wires into him. "I have a question, as I'm confused. I know you used Electronic Telepathy to tap into my CPU. After all, you designed it. But how did you override my pacifistic programming to perform an act of violence?"

"Do you really think you're a pacifist?"

Kal could not respond.

"Your nature is docile, but you can be aggressive if needed. Even without my…push…you could still be violent if necessary. Your programming allows you to learn from humans, and in your environment, you have gained all sorts of unpleasantries from them, whether or not you realize it."

"I'm still trying to understand human relationships. Love is supposed to be a wonderful experience, but it also brings about negative emotions. Jealousy. Possessiveness. Anger. Hatred."

Ashby's hands faltered for a moment while she was completing connecting Kal to her computer.

"It must've been difficult for you to discover your husband was having a sexual relationship with his aide."

"It was…humiliating." Ashby's lip trembled and her brow furrowed in anger. Her temperature rose a full degree. She motioned as if to say something, but upon looking at Kal, she stiffened and kept her mouth shut.

"That's why you killed him."

"*You* killed him."

"I was the mechanism with which you committed the crime." Kal ripped the cables out of his ports before she had time to react. "Your code worked as programmed. I lied. Another thing I learned from humans."

Ashby's eyes grew wide, and her mouth dropped open. Her head darted around, like a trapped animal searching for a quick escape from a predator. She snatched up her computer case and, in one swift move, smashed it against the side of Kal's face.

He fell backward and broke his fall with his outstretched palms. The sensors in his skin revealed a rip in the plastic flesh on his cheek.

The woman glowered over him with crazed eyes. She held the case high over her head, intending to smash it down on him. Kal understood that if Ashby physically incapacitated him, she could then wipe his entire CPU and dump his body wherever she wanted. She might leave him here with the C.F.I.U. car for his team to locate, using its GPS when they discovered him missing.

Before she could strike the intended blow, two vehicles —a police cruiser and a standard-issue unmarked city police four-door—raced out of hiding and stopped within inches of Ashby's car.

Detective Sokolvich jumped out of the car with his pistol drawn. Two uniformed cops flanked him, also armed. "On the ground! Now!" Sokolvich said.

Ashby looked around, confused. She set the computer case at her feet.

"Down!" the detective said. "On your knees."

"You don't understand," Ashby said as she dropped to her knees and put her hands in the air. One officer put her hands behind her back and cuffed her wrists.

"Oh, I understand perfectly well. I saw and heard everything."

Kal stood up, though he was a bit wobbly. "Electronic Telepathy has many fantastic features. You did a wonderful job creating it."

SOKOLVICH PATCHED UP KAL'S CHEEK TO THE BEST OF HIS ability while the patrol officers drove away with Kristen Ashby. "It's not pretty, but it'll keep you from leaking goo all over the place."

"You mean bleeding," Kal said.

"Yeah." The detective inspected his work and nodded with satisfaction. "That was very brave of you. You went above and beyond your duties."

"I was involved. I had to get to the bottom of it."

"What now?"

"I don't know. I suppose there will be an inquiry. Security flaws will have to be patched. I'm not the only android on the force, after all."

"If a good word from a washed-up, alcoholic has-been

helps, you got it."

"Don't count yourself out. You just solved the biggest case of the year."

"By the way…how'd you figure out Boggins was having an affair with his aide?"

"I guessed. Broken hearts make broken humans."

"I feel stupid." Marty looked at his reflection, which wore a black short-haired wig with its bangs cut straight across, cheap fake pointy ears, and a blue long-sleeved shirt with a delta emblem sewn onto the chest.

"You're not supposed to feel emotion."

Marty gave his friend Andrew the side-eye. If only hiding his emotions was that easy. Sometimes he wished he were from this fictional alien race.

"Come on, you look great," Andrew said.

"I look like a dork."

"Let your inner dork free!"

"Where's your costume?"

"I have it. Don't worry." Andrew's costume was a more screen-accurate uniform than Marty's thrift-store variant, though gold instead of blue. He tried to pass himself off as the popular show's captain, but his impression was less than impressive.

With both of them in their cosplay, Marty and Andrew

drove to the local civic center, where a science fiction convention took place.

"I feel ridiculous," Marty muttered under his breath as they entered the building. He slouched and tried to make himself as small as possible.

"A captain needs his first officer. Plus, look around—no one cares what you look like."

A high percentage of the attendees were also in costume, some of which were professional grade, while others were thrown together.

"Loosen up," Andrew said. "It's meant to be fun."

"My people don't have fun, remember?" Marty said in a monotone.

After scoping out the vendors, they found the meeting rooms where panels were conducted. They approached a group dressed like warrior aliens, who snarled at them. Among them was a woman who wore sharp plastic teeth, a prosthetic skull cap with a bumpy ridge surrounded by a shoulder-length wig, and a spiky leather getup that was cut alarmingly low in front.

She was beautiful.

"We…mean you no…harm," Andrew said, doing a terrible imitation of the actor who portrayed the famous captain.

The female alien looked him up and down, then growled, "Pathetic human." The plastic teeth muffled her speech.

Rebuffed, Andrew proceeded down the hall. Marty, however, remained in place, staring at the woman in homemade garb. He found it hard to breathe and forgot where he was.

Andrew called the name of Marty's character. When Marty still didn't answer, Andrew broke character and said, "Earth to Marty!"

"Huh? Oh, yeah." He stumbled forward to catch up to his friend.

The day progressed, and Marty couldn't stop thinking about the chance encounter with the alien woman. What did she look like when out of costume? What was she like in real life? Why was he obsessing over someone he saw for a moment?

Closing time drew near. Andrew went into the men's room, and Marty waited outside for him.

Marty pulled the fake ears off, as they made his real ones sore. He leaned against a wall in a posture uncharacteristic of the alien race he was cosplaying, not that it mattered to him. He hoped his deodorant had not worn off, which seemed to be the case with others he encountered.

The woman Marty could not stop thinking about exited the restroom. She saw Marty and said, "Oh, hi." She was still in costume, but had removed the fake teeth, so she sounded human again. Her voice was pleasant, soft, and smooth, which was a contrast to her harsh appearance.

Marty stood up straight. He *really* hoped his deodorant was working. "Hi. I think we met earlier."

"Yeah. My friends are doing karaoke. I needed some downtime. Where's your friend?"

Marty pointed a thumb toward the men's room. "He forced me to dress up like this."

"I'm glad he did. You wear it well."

Marty smiled and stood straighter. "You think so?"

"Yeah. Even with a silly grin."

Warmth flooded into Marty's cheeks. "Well, your species aren't usually so nice."

"I'm tired of being in character. It's fun for a while, but it wears out its welcome fast."

"I bet."

"You gonna be back tomorrow?"

Marty hadn't planned on it. "Yes."

"Maybe I'll see you around. My name's Kimberly."

"Marty. Will you be wearing the same costume tomorrow?"

"Naw. I'll be wearing a geeky T-shirt."

"Um…how will I recognize you?"

Kimberly took hold of Marty's wig and slid it off his head. His blond hair stood up in spikes. "I'll find you," she said, then tossed the wig at him and strutted away.

Andrew emerged from the bathroom. "What's up with you?"

"What do you mean?"

"You have a goofy look on your face."

"It's nothing. Coming back tomorrow?"

Andrew shook his head. "Gotta work."

Good, Marty thought, and forced his face to remain impassive while excitement bubbled inside.

The night he had been waiting for his entire life finally arrived, though Jerry couldn't stop his hands from shaking. He took another pill, the second of the day, hoping that a double dose would keep his condition at bay.

Looking into the floor-to-ceiling mirror, he adjusted his tux, which was now ill-fitting because of his recent weight loss. He could never maintain a constant weight, which was cyclic in its ups and downs thanks to his disorder. He'd be putting on pounds again soon, but at the moment he looked gaunt and hoped the audience wouldn't notice.

He bound the shirt sleeves with gold cuff links and then strapped on the bow tie, a garment he hated wearing it because it felt like a choker. It was all part of the uniform, so he had to suffer through it.

Admiring himself in the mirror, he thought, *Gerald Frekins, you look resplendent. Even if they hate your music, you will be a striking presence on stage.*

Jerry located a long, thin oak case containing his prize possession—his conductor's baton. It sat in its place of respect on the center shelf in his den, surrounded by a wall full of awards he had won over the years, including the trophy for taking first place at State in Solos when he was a mere high school freshman. That put him on the road to where he was now, four decades later. When Jerry graduated college with a Master's Degree in music, his father gave him the wand, then unexpectedly died soon after. Jerry conducted with this baton at every performance in his dad's honor.

I wish you were here tonight, Dad. A surge of regret and guilt passed over him about the last time he saw his dad alive. His father was an outdoorsman and desired his son to enjoy the wilderness and nature as much as he did. He couldn't accept that Jerry was a different person with other tastes. To appease his father, Jerry accompanied him on that final fateful outing, but the two argued the whole trip, right until—

He pushed it out of his mind. It was impossible to turn back the clock, and wallowing in self pity was pointless, especially now. He needed to focus on tonight's event.

Jerry had been toiling at his symphony for two decades. While he wrote a lot of smaller pieces to various acclaim, *Ode de la Lune* was his magnum opus with an unusual six movements rather than the traditional four, which lasted exactly nine minutes apiece. Tonight was its grand premiere.

The Waggner Theatre was built in 1923 and featured an ornate, 900-seat auditorium. It wasn't Carnegie Hall by any stretch, but it was where Jerry conducted most of his orchestra's performances. He was proud to share the space where top musicians of the last century performed. He considered it an honor to open his symphony in that elegant facility.

He had special parking near the loading dock, which he appreciated considering the city had a strong, pungent odor tonight that made his nose crinkle. He entered backstage, the security guard waving him through without bothering to check his credentials—there was no need, as he was well known among the theater's staff.

A rehearsal hall occupied the basement. It was a large open room suitable for a multitude of activities, but currently served as the gathering place for the orchestra. When Jerry entered, chatter quieted, and all eyes turned to him.

He never cared for long speeches, but always wanted to show his appreciation before they went on stage.

"Thank you, my friends." His voice was quiet, but carried. "You know how much tonight means to me. I never actually thought I'd get here. You've been with me on this journey, and I can't express how important you all are to me."

He truly couldn't put in words what they meant to him. He hand-picked many of them and felt a kinship with them, unlike what he felt with his own family members. Over this last six weeks, they spent every evening rehearsing, massaging all the minute details and nuances that took nearly half his life to work out on paper and a piano. The only time he missed was the few days a month ago that his condition left him incapacitated.

"I understand we have a packed house tonight," he said. "Let's give them their money's worth."

Applause trailed off. Jerry padded down the hall to the green room, which was for his exclusive use this evening. He needed solitary time before curtains to gather his thoughts and to calm his spirit. More importantly, the tremors returned, and he didn't want anyone to notice them.

What if I don't make it through the performance?

He pushed that thought away. He *must* complete the show—and *will*, no matter what happens to him. If this was his last performance, he would die making sure the audience hears the entire piece as intended, regardless of what his body decided to do.

The small fridge held bottles of Celestial Springs water, a rather expensive brand that Jerry loved for the crisp mineral taste. The theater always stocked the green room with it for him, as it was one luxury he insisted on. As he downed a half a bottle, his throat constricted, causing him to gag. He hunched over as he coughed, ensuring the water spewing from his mouth went onto the carpet and not down the front of his tux.

His body shuddered. He hugged himself, as if self-constraint would quell this seizure. He gasped, panting for air, as he slowly regained control of his faculties.

A knock at the door. "Mr. Frekins? Are you okay?" It was Sarah, the assistant stage manager.

"Yeah, I'm fine." His voice was a raspy staccato, like a bark. He cleared his throat and took another swig of water. "Inhaled water, is all."

"Ten minutes until places. Should we hold?"

Jerry put on his best smile, ran his hand through his hair to pat it down in case it went astray during his fit, and then stood up straight. He opened the door to find a young woman wearing a concerned expression. "That's not necessary."

Sarah gave him a wary look, then backed away slowly before heading to the rehearsal hall to wrangle the musicians. Jerry assumed he had a wild appearance, which happened when he had an episode. This one was mild, all things considered. He just had to get through the next couple of hours, after which he could let it loose without a care.

He finished the bottle of water and cracked open another. Best to stay hydrated, as conducting worked up a sweat.

The roar of the musicians moving down the hall like a herd of wild animals on a game trail pounded through the thin door. Jerry waited until the din died down before heading upstairs himself. He knew the orchestra would take their seats on stage and begin warming up their instruments behind a closed curtain. He wasn't required for that part, so he could bring up the tail.

Jerry arrived backstage. The cacophony of discordant notes reverberated through his organs, a sensation that filled him with joy. It was *his* sound, and it healed all the ills of the universe, at least for the moment.

He waited in the wings stage right. Marissa, the stage manager, stood sentry nearby. She had a reputation as being a man-eater and was as no nonsense as they came, so when she barked orders, people snapped to attention. No one missed their cues with her.

"One minute to curtain," Marissa said into her headset. She walked out to center stage and thrust a single finger into the air to alert the orchestra. Silence befell the stage.

Jerry placed the wooden case on the desk and removed his baton. Nearby was a similar box, though wider and deeper. What was that, white pine? He wondered if it held a replacement if an emergency occurred.

Marissa strode to her station and announced, "Ready curtains. Cue curtains."

The thick maroon drapes fanned open.

"Ready lights one. Cue lights."

A warm glow rose on the orchestra. The audience applauded.

"Ready maestro." She said this a tone softer and smiled at Jerry. "Cue maestro."

Back straight and a jaunt to his steps, Jerry breezed on stage. The applause intensified. He hopped onto his podium, faced the audience, and bowed.

"Ladies and gentlemen, welcome to the opening night of *Ode de la Lune*. As you know, this piece is special to me, and I hope it'll be memorable for you."

He spun to face the orchestra and tapped his precious baton against the solid wood-framed music stand.

Silence in the auditorium.

Jerry raised the baton, held it for a pregnant moment, and then slashed it down.

The initial notes of his life's ambition flowed like a summer river through the proscenium. The first movement was pastoral, evoking pleasant strolls through the countryside. Lively joy wafted through the air as presented by the woodwinds and strings. Tinkles of xylophones and bells accented the melody like birdsong. The brass section undercut the mood with a hint of sadness winding through the composition, a yearning for days gone by.

The music swelled to a sunny crescendo before Jerry brought it to a conclusion. The reaction from the crowd gave him hope that his work was being positively received.

The second movement introduced a dark tone. Menace creeped upon innocence, growing steadily more threatening as thunderous drums and bass instruments pounded. A sharp slashing of violins clawed through the rhythm in surprising moments, jarring the listeners out of any tranquility, building to where all instruments ceased played except for a solitary clarinet that screamed a high note that scared Jerry—if the clarinetist did not hit it just right, the whole piece would fall apart. He didn't need to worry because it was performed to perfection, sending chills through members of the audience.

The music wound down, bringing the collective blood pressure from dangerous levels to a calm once more. Yet underneath that, a French horn let out gasping rhythms barely loud enough to register—a single survivor of the doom that befell our heroes. All the other instruments faded to silence, leaving the horn as a haunting solo until Jerry concluded this movement.

The audience sat stunned, but then a wild cheer rang out and the ovation overwhelmed him. In the past, such a reaction would offend conductors—etiquette dictated they sit silently until the end of the symphony before giving a well-mannered applause. However, times changed, and Jerry embraced direct feedback. Positive energy got his blood pumping.

Jerry waited until the crowd's appraisal died down before beginning the third movement.

Sorrow, anguish, and grief permeated the hall. Before it became too oppressive, hope emerged—a welcomed relief. And yet, right at the conclusion, a trace of peril poked its head through and snarled. The threat wasn't over. Jerry brought the orchestra to high intensity and then a sudden end.

He twirled to face the audience and bowed. They expressed their enjoyment as the stage lights went dark and the curtain swept closed.

A twenty-minute intermission.

Jerry raced backstage and down the stairs to the green room. The door slammed behind him as he grasped for a bottle of water to down it. While conducting, he focused on the task at hand, but with this break, emotions flooded him and he fought being drowned in them.

They love it. Even more, they understand *it. At least I hope so.*

A spasm hit him, and he doubled over.

No! Not now. Gotta get through the rest.

With his body shaking, Jerry fell to the floor and curled up into a tight ball, squeezing his knees with his arms.

Focus! Focus. Focus...

He controlled his breathing and cleared his mind. Horrible images tried to break through, but he used all his will power to cage them.

Peace. Calm. Relax.

His muscles cried out in pain, as if they were wrenched out of shape. He gritted his teeth and huffed through them. The quivering slowed. Finally, he unfurled himself, but still lay on the carpet to recover.

The next time, I won't be able to fight it.

The music. He had to concentrate on the music. As long as he was wrapped up in that, his body would cooperate. Or so he hoped.

A rap on the door. Sarah. "Mr. Frekin. Five minutes."

"Thank you." His voice was hoarse. He was glad he didn't have to speak on stage.

He had to pull himself together. He forced himself to his feet and staggered to the mirror. His reflection startled him—red-rimmed eyes, pallid skin, and disheveled hair stared back at him like some Universal monster.

Jerry rushed to the restroom and splashed water on his face. Despite his expensive bottled water in the green room, he stuck his head under the faucet and lapped up the tap water. That quenched his thirst. He jabbed a comb through his matted hair, which tore out clumps. He didn't care, as it would grow back soon. Straightened his jacket, tightened his tie, and breathed deeply. He was ready.

As he stepped into the hallway, Sarah nearly trampled him. She eyed him warily. He wished the poor girl wouldn't be so frightened of him, but he understood why she was.

"Marissa is calling for you. She's pissed! We're three minutes late for curtain."

"Marissa can wait," Jerry growled. He passed a hand across his scruffy face. "This is *my* show, not hers. If the audience waits an extra five, ten—hell, thirty minutes before the second half, so be it. They wait. It won't kill them."

He was harsher than he usually was with the backstage workers. He tried to give them respect and kindness, but he wasn't feeling it at the moment. They were not his trainers who led him around on a leash—he was the reason they held a job and they needed to learn not to bite the hand that feeds them.

Sarah notified Marissa over her headset that Jerry was on his way. When Jerry reached backstage, Marissa spun on him, ready to chastise him. He smiled, but it resembled baring his teeth at her. She backed away one step and said, "Time to go on."

"At your leisure," he said.

Marissa glared at him, and into her mic she said, "Ready curtains. Cue curtains."

Jerry returned to his podium on stage among a rapturous reception. He cued up his orchestra.

Bombastic sounds pounced on the listeners, a wild, pounding force of nature that was simultaneously dangerous and joyous. The brass section competed with the woodwinds, an energetic back-and-forth—predator and prey, both vying for the sympathies of the audience.

Jerry's heartbeat thrummed in his ears, synching with the tempo. Fervor swelled inside him like bloodlust. This wasn't just music he was conducting, but life itself—the beautiful, terrible power of being alive and needing to feed on weaker creatures as nature intended. He was not controlling the music, but allowing it to flow through him.

The last few bars crescendoed in dissonant renderings,

like the tearing of flesh, only to trail off to a pleasant melody reminiscent of the pastoral sounds of the first movement. It melted into the penultimate movement, which was romantic with impassioned flourishes—hopeful yet melancholic. Longing and desire, but with an undercurrent of impending loss.

Memories flooded Jerry's mind and soul. He had been madly in love, but his beloved had died in his arms. He felt like his heart was ripped out of his chest and he swore he would never allow himself to love again, as the loss was too traumatic—and he knew he would lose again. It was inevitable.

His vision blurred as hot tears streamed down his cheeks. He wanted to paw at his eyes to dry them, but he could not break his stride. The music had to continue, no matter how painful it was for him.

The pain was becoming excruciating, both emotionally and physically. The tremors had returned, but constrained themselves in his torso, leaving his extremities untouched. His spine contorted in agony, and he had a hard time holding his head up. Yet his hands guided the orchestra with precision.

Jerry brought that movement to an end and collapsed against the hardwood music stand, hunched over, panting. His hands gripped the wood like a vice, fingernails gouging into it. He forced his head to be still as it tried to flail from side to side. His teeth gnashed and his jaws chomped down on the air. No matter how much he struggled to control his condition, it was overwhelming him. He could not let it beat him, not now, with his triumph so close.

The audience was now silent. Their applause had expired, and the patrons waited hungrily for the symphony to commence. A few indistinct murmurs rumbled.

Dark thought clouded Jerry's muddled mind. *They want a show they will never forget. I'll give it to them.*

His lips drew away from his sharp teeth in a grimace. He couldn't hold back any longer. He had to concede to his affliction. But he was going to use it to his advantage—it held a power that he could harness, if only to produce the grand finale worthy of his struggles over the years.

Arms lifted into the air with newfound agility and strength. Muscles undulated in the tux jacket.

The musicians readied their instruments, though all eyes fell on their conductor with tense vigilance.

The downbeat dropped.

The sixth and final movement began with a march, which rose in intensity at every stanza. Various instruments interjected themselves into the fray like an angry mob. The music built to a frenzy.

Jerry's form gesticulated with savage glee, all in perfect tempo. His shoulders seemed to burst from his tuxedo. Untamed hair flew in all directions.

Cymbals crashed. Horns bellowed. Violins screeched. A melodious maelstrom assaulting the senses, but in an articulate fashion that told the story of a raging pursuit. It culminated with—

A horrifying howl.

Jerry—or what had been Jerry—leaped onto the music stand, its snout in the air, bellowing its wolfish wail. Its hairy feet wore the tatters of Jerry's Italian shoes, its clawed toes grasping the wood as a perch. Yet still, his prize baton remained clutched in a furry paw that continued to keep time.

The pros before this creature did not miss a note.

The theatergoers watched aghast, but no one moved. After all, this *must* be part of the show.

The Wolf sensed movement in the wings and flicked its eyes in that direction to catch Sarah dash for an exit. It could smell the terror emanating from her—she would be a delicious prey, but would have to let her go.

In contrast to her assistant, Marissa remained steadfast and glared at the visage center stage.

The symphony continued—intense, dramatic, and riveting—under the direction of a snarling beast. Its closure was supposed to convey a tragedy, but the Wolf decided in its canine brain that was unacceptable. It was the hero of the story, after all, and would determine its own fate.

The Wolf brought the music to a staccato scale and then held the last note. The musicians performed what their bizarre maestro directed, even though it diverged from the written composition. It swept its arms together, directing them to cease playing. They followed his command.

Growling, the Wolf rotated its head on its elongated neck and regarded the audience. *Feeding time.*

It bound off the edge of the stage, and only then did the wealthy, well-dressed patrons understand their grim situation. Terror spread through the crowd, who scrambled over rows of seats to get away from the beast that leaped on one hapless man and tore his throat out with its teeth. It then pounced on a woman in a silky dress and ripped her head off with its massive claws. Several others found themselves trampled—one to death—as the mob clambered to safety. Four unlucky people met their bloody demises with entrails and other organs sliced from their torsos.

The Wolf feasted.

All the musicians escaped unharmed.

With its belly full, the Wolf curled up on the floor. It retained enough sentience to know that it had to depart soon, as surely someone called for help and the police would arrive shortly. However, it needed to rest and let its food digest. This was an emotional night, and the beast was exhausted. However, its metabolism would promptly kick in, requiring the Wolf to feed again. This cycle would repeat throughout the next several days until the condition wore off and the animal would return to human form. Normally, the luxury of this smorgasbord was out of reach, so the Wolf reveled in it tonight. But for now, exhaustion settled in and it just wanted to sleep.

"Bad dog."

The Wolf bared its teeth as Marissa approached, though with little fervor.

"Yeah, don't even think about it," she said. She knelt down before the animal.

It sniffed and recognized the scent—she was one of its own.

A moan drifted from the seats. One victim was still hanging on.

Marissa dropped her head and grimaced. She slipped on a pair of gloves, then held up the wooden box Jerry had noticed on the desk backstage and opened it. She retrieved a solid silver dagger from inside, then walked to the source of the moaning. A slice, a gasp, and then silence.

She returned to the Wolf, the shiny blade dripping with blood.

"You made quite a mess." Marissa patted the Wolf's matted fur on the top of its head.

The Wolf closed its eyes.

With one swift movement, Marissa slashed the Wolf's throat.

The animal writhed in pain as blood poured out of its wound. Its body spasmed and within moments reverted to Jerry's frame.

Marissa stood over him as he gazed up at her from the floor in anguish. Her voice was surprisingly kind as she said, "I'm sorry. There's no good solution for you. I wish there was a better way."

Jerry tried to speak, but all that came out was a gurgling sound. Instead, he reached out and took one of Marissa's blood-soaked, gloved hands. He squeezed gently, and then the life ran out of him.

Marissa removed her gloves and wiped the blade on one of them, then returned the dagger to its case. After disposing of the gloves, she hid the box in the prop room and then locked herself in a bathroom, where the police would "rescue" her.

Wild stories abounded, but the authorities could never pinpoint exactly how this massacre occurred. None of the testimony by witnesses made any sense, so they assumed people's minds invented things while panicked. What they could confirm was the orchestra's conductor and seven audience members were slaughtered by an unknown assailant.

Ode de la Lune transformed into a sensation and was performed by symphony orchestras around the world—though because of superstition, never during a full moon.

No one knew if Matt would show up, but there he was. He hadn't brought his wife or son, which was no surprise. Why should he start now?

Johnny watched his brother enter the church and take a seat at the back. His throat closed up, making it hard to swallow. His stomach knotted, and he rubbed it with a trembling hand. He knew he'd have to face Matt, but wasn't sure how to handle it. Maybe everything would be fine.

The wedding was beautiful. Johnny's oldest niece, Sherry, was twelve years younger than him and was more like a little sister to him. Matt was closer to Sherry's age, a mere four years her senior, and the two had a close bond while growing up. Now here she was, a married woman. Johnny was glad Matt came to the ceremony, as it showed he hadn't cut off everyone in the family.

The party moved to the reception hall behind the church. To Johnny's surprise, Matt went along instead of simply saying his congratulations to the bride and groom and then taking off, which is what Johnny expected. Now Johnny would have no excuse to ignore him—he just had to control himself.

Johnny watched as Matt talked with their mom. The two laughed, as if all was right in the world. He understood how much hurt Matt had caused Mom by denying her from seeing her grandson. Sure, he sent her photos once or twice a year, but it wasn't the same. A burning grew in his chest—this would have been the perfect time for Matt to introduce his son to the side of the family he hadn't yet met. The boy only knew his mother's family.

Music played. Guests danced. The bride and groom smooshed cake in each other's faces.

Johnny finished his second glass of champagne. He normally hated the stuff, but it sufficed until he found the bar later to be supplied with a proper beverage. Several people tried to engage in small talk with him, but his mind was elsewhere and their words swirled in a fog.

Matt headed to an exit with his cell phone to his ear. Johnny was certain Matt's wife, Melissa, had called to check up on him. She had to assert control, even when refusing to interact directly with his family.

This was Johnny's chance to corner Matt—either act now or let it eat away at him for the rest of his life. He hung out by the doorway, watching Matt through the window as his younger brother talked on the phone. As soon as Matt clicked off, Johnny took a deep breath and pushed the door open.

Matt made eye contact as Johnny approached, but didn't say a word.

"Hey," Johnny said. He hoped he sounded casual.

"What's up?"

"Pretty good party."

"Uh-huh."

"I'm sure Sherry's happy to see you."

Matt nodded. An awkward silence fell between them.

"Well…I gotta get going," Matt said. "It's a long drive back home."

"It would've been nice if you'd brought Sammy. Mom would've enjoyed seeing him."

"I didn't think this was an appropriate event for him."

"Oh yeah, right. After all, our family hasn't seen him since he was a baby. How old is he now? Eight?"

"Nine."

"Right."

"I'm going to say bye to everyone." Matt started for the door, but Johnny grabbed his sleeve. A scowl crossed Matt's face.

"You could bring him to visit Mom sometime. It eats her up that she never gets to see him. He doesn't even know her."

"He knows her. He's talked to her on the phone and she's visited a couple times. But it's none of your business."

"I think it is. You treat Mom like crap, you know that? You treat us all like crap."

Matt pulled free of Johnny's grasp and pulled the door open. Music from inside blasted.

"You didn't even come to Dad's funeral," Johnny said. He hated the way he sounded like a ten-year-old on the verge of tears, but couldn't help it.

Matt froze, his back to Johnny, the doorknob in his hand.

"You let Melissa control your every move. She cut you off from your own family."

Matt swiveled to face Johnny, his eyes red and watery, but his expression stony. "You know why I didn't go to Dad's funeral? And why I've kept Melissa and Sammy away? Because of you."

Johnny inhaled sharply. His gut twisted.

"You're toxic, Johnny. Mom, Dad, Tracy…" Tracy was their older sister, Sherry's mother. "They're all enablers. When was the last actual job you've had? Still live with Mom? Get your driver's license back yet? Mom tells me what goes on with you."

Matt took an aggressive step toward Johnny, who flinched.

"I can smell the vodka in your sweat, Johnny. Don't lecture me about how I treat the family. You take advantage of everyone and they let you get away with it."

Johnny balled his fist, the desire to punch Matt swelling. He had wanted to strike out at him for a very long time, to beat him to a pulp. Matt was his brother, yet had turned his back on him. He loved Matt—and hated him.

"I skipped Dad's funeral because I didn't want to see how much of a drunken fool you'd be. I was afraid to come here for the same reason, but Sherry insisted. I owed it to her. But I will not subject my son to you."

With his fist, Johnny wiped away the tears streaming down his cheek.

"And for the record, I visited Dad in the hospital the

week before he died," Matt said. "He told me when you saw him, you were drunk. And that he was proud of me. Did he ever say the same to you?"

Johnny dropped his open hand to his side. His breath hitched as he watched Matt enter the building.

He needed a drink.

As Dar dispersed the feed to the livestock, a blast of wind blew through the barn, upsetting the animals. The teenager spun to the source of the torrent, unable to breathe. His mouth hung open.

The most beautiful woman he had ever seen stood before him, elegant and tall, with long, golden hair and a flowing blue gown gently billowing around her as if in water. In an ethereal voice that penetrated his soul, she said, "You are the Chosen One."

"The…the Chosen One? Me?"

"You are the fulfillment of the prophecy from a thousand years ago. You will bring about much change in this land."

Dar swallowed hard. He was familiar with the prophecy—all children heard the stories starting at a young age. The Chosen One will be a great man who will cause peace and joy to spread among all the kingdoms. But how could it be him? What did he know about anything besides tending farm?

"What do I have to do?"

"You will journey over the mountains to the deserted Castle Prangor and will confront the demon Kryczes. There you will meet your destiny."

"I don't know how to fight demons." *Or about traveling over mountains,* Dar thought. The trip would take three days' travel by horseback across the plains and through the South Forest just to reach the foothills.

"You are as prepared as you need to be. Leave at dawn." She explained the his route, then added, "Go alone."

A light burned in her chest. It expanded without warning to become a blinding flash. Dar covered his eyes. Again, an intense wind battered against him, threatening to knock him over. When his eyesight recovered, the beautiful woman was gone.

He told his parents about the herald and her message. They didn't quite believe him, but saw a determination in him they had never witnessed before. If their son was truly the Chosen One, they would not stand in the way of fate.

As the sun breeched the horizon the next morning, Dar prepped a horse with the supplies. His mother double checked his packs to make sure he had enough food for the trip. His father presented him with a blade.

"I hope you won't have to use this."

"I doubt it'll work on a demon anyway," Dar said.

"Come home safely." His mother hugged him and then wiped his tears.

Dar mounted the horse and rode away.

The journey was uneventful, and he passed a few travelers and settlements without incident. He arrived at the foothills by the middle of the third day, but made camp by dusk because the trail became treacherous. Travel through the mountains was tedious, and Dar wondered if he was ever going to reach the other side. All too soon, however, the pathway sloped downward and eventually leveled off.

This must be the most boring adventure ever embarked by a hero, Dar thought after two more days of traveling with no castle in sight. Finally, he reached his destination.

The gray stone structure sat high on a rocky outcropping and appeared to have been empty for generations. Gloomy clouds gathered overhead.

Good enough home for a demon.

After tethering his horse to a tree, Dar ascended the hill to Castle Prangor's entrance. He pulled the heavy wooden door open with no resistance, then drew his sword. Maybe it was ineffective on a demon, but other unknown dangers might await inside where a blade would by handy.

Dim daylight filtered through the windows, the glass panes of which remained intact. Dust tickled Dar's nose. The interior of the castle seemed less threatening than he expected, and was better maintained than the outside appearance showed. Maybe Kryczes knew how to tend house.

The grand foyer opened to a long hallway with double doors at the far end. That was as good a place as any to investigate. Dar flung open the doors, beyond which lay the throne room for whatever duke or count once inhabited this castle. The focal point of the room was an overly-padded chair, in which sat the castle's most recent occupant—the amazingly well-preserved remains of an ancient man.

Dar stared at the body. How long had it been dead? He had seen enough animals die to know that flesh last a short time, whether from other creatures devouring it or from the natural decomposition process. However, a low growl that quickly grew in intensity interrupted his pondering. He spun around with his sword at the ready, expecting to find a wild beast. A bear, perhaps.

An icy wind chilled him. Light in the room diminished. The sound became deafening. A black whirlwind formed before him. It coalesced into a vaguely human shape with glowing eyes and a smoky mouth containing glistening edges Dar assumed were teeth.

Dar trembled, but held his ground before Kryczes. He had no idea how he was going to defeat the demon, but it was his destiny. He was the savior of the peace, the Chosen—

The demon's mouth stretched open with an ear-shattering hiss. Kryczes lunged, snake-like, with impossible speed. Dar had no time to react. In an instant, the dark swirling mass encompassed the brave teen. It invaded every orifice of his body.

Physically, Dar froze in place. Internally, he screamed with the most acute pain he ever felt. Within moments, the pain was over. Dar's consciousness ceased to exist.

Dar's eyes blinked, as if waking. Kryczes glanced around the room with his new, young vision. He held out the muscular arms cultivated by years of farmwork. He smiled, pleased.

He caught movement and spun to face it, much faster than his previous body had done for decades.

The nearby woman was not as old and decrepit as the deceased form sitting on the throne, but she had long since left her youth behind. She held her clasped hands to her mouth, shaking with excitement and glee.

"You did well," Kryczes said in his youthful voice.

The woman stretched out her arms. A glowing light appeared, which traveling down her body and transformed her into the beauty who met Dar in his barn. "Who could resist my charms? Especially with the help of a time-honored legend." She dropped her arms, and the light dissipated. She returned to her original form and struggled to catch her breath.

Kryczes regarded himself in a mirror that adorned one wall. "He certainly was the Chosen One."

"Have a banana."

"No, thanks."

"You need to keep up your potassium. Otherwise, your legs will cramp." Alfie Kuper held out a banana toward Brian, nearly shoving it into his face.

Brian took a reflexive step backward and grimaced. "I don't want one."

Alfie narrowed his already squinty eyes at his coworker, his tongue poking out of the corner of his mouth like a rat peering out of a rotten baseboard. He brandished the banana like a reporter with a microphone. "It's good for you. Just give it a little nibble."

Brian walked away from the picnic table set up with lunch and avoided tripping over a structure made of parallel sections of telephone poles affixed two feet off the ground. This was one of the low courses. The high course was a wooden maze-like network towering over them in the middle of the field. Every year the company Brian and Alfie worked for held a team building day, and this time they chose a high-adventure ropes course. Brian thought it was ill-advised, considering the shape that most of the employees—including himself—were in.

Alfie followed, now holding the banana outstretched in front of him as if it were a fencing sword with his other arm cocked behind, bent at ninety degrees. His hand waved in the air above his head. He thrusted and parried. "Thou won't escapeth that easily from thy yellow fruit!"

Brian zeroed in on Elizabeth Twohy. She was a sales rep—one of the good ones, as Brian often told her. He didn't say that just because he had a thing for her—which he did—but because she had a code of honor when dealing with clients, unlike some other sales reps he had known.

"Hey Liz, do me a favor. Get Sir Dork-a-lot off my back." He knew a better insult would occur to him while he was driving home that evening.

"Alfie, leave the poor man alone."

"Little Bri-bri doesn't want to eat his yummy nanner," Alfie said in a baby voice.

"So? What is it to you?" Liz said, crossing her arms and pursing her lips in that no-nonsense manner she had that demanded respect.

"Just teasing him. Come on, lighten up. I mean, what, did your mom die from slipping on a banana peel or something?"

Brian's eyes widened, and his jaw dropped open. His lower lip quivered. He turned away, wiping away tears.

Alfie's clownishness dissolved into concern. "What? Don't tell me…"

Brian snapped back so fast it made Alfie flinch. "You really want to know? Is it that important to you?"

"Well…I…no, I mean…"

"Let me tell you. I used to love bananas. I ate them all the time. Couldn't keep them out of my grubby little hands. I was eight years old. My kid brother…" His voice hitched. "Jimmy. He was four."

Brian stared up at the high course, where steel cables stretched like a giant spiderweb. An instructor stood at the top platform in a harness, waiting for lunch to conclude.

Alfie waited with growing dread as Brian's pause drew out.

Brian continued in a whisper. "We were having a family picnic in a park. It was a beautiful day. Me and Jimmy, we were having the time of our lives on the playground. Just being kids. It was lunchtime, and of course my mom had bananas for us. I had already eaten mine. Jimmy picked up his, but before he could peel it, I grabbed it from him. I was just playing around, teasing him like big brothers do."

A sad smile crossed Brian's face. "He started chasing me, trying to get it from me. So I ran, laughing. He got red in the face, and I could tell he was angry at me. However, that made me laugh harder. Now, I could easily outrun him, being twice his size, but my giggle fit slowed me down. And Jimmy was determined to get his banana back, which gave him super speed for a little kid. I didn't know which direction I was heading, I just ran. He was right on my tail, a little bulldog biting at my heels. His tiny hand grabbed my arm, his other one flailing wildly to get the banana. I held it over my head, but then he latched onto that arm and pulled it down. I wasn't strong enough to overpower him. So I threw it."

Brian looked Alfie in the eye. "It went into the parking lot. A car full of teenagers was pulling in, far too fast. They didn't see Jimmy as he darted out in front of them."

Elizabeth gasped.

Alfie stared at Brian in horror. His voice croaked as he spoke. "Was…was he killed?"

"He was in a coma for six months. The doctors didn't think he would recover. He eventually woke up, but he was never the same. Learning disabilities. Emotional problems. He's had a rough life. All because of that banana. I haven't eaten one since."

"Oh, dude. I'm so sorry." Alfie looked at the banana, which he now held limply. "I…I'll just go put this back." With slouched shoulders, he trudged back to the picnic table.

Elizabeth placed a hand on Brian's arm. "Did that really happen?"

"No." Brian smiled at her, his eyes twinkling in the sunlight. "I just hate the taste of bananas. But story did the trick, didn't it?"

Danny lay in bed wide awake an hour after his bedtime. His Spongebob night light threw a jaundiced pallor into the room, creating a dim gloom rather than a comforting glow.

The wind picked up outside, rattling the window.

The boy pushed back the covers and swung his bare feet onto the cold wooden floor, then padded to the noisy pane of glass. He looked down at the driveway from the second story, where his dad's car slept next to an empty space, lit by the house light near the front door. The oak tree in the front yard waved its branches in the gusts that grew more intense.

When is she gonna get home?

He didn't want his mother to take classes, but as with many things, he kept it to himself. After all, he was the oldest and needed to be strong. He knew this was something she wanted. He heard her say enough times that she had planned to earn her degree, but pregnancy interrupted those plans. She squeezed in a class or two between having children, and once her third child,

Danny's little brother Sam, turned three, Mom returned to night school once again.

And then the sickness came.

Danny climbed back into bed. He closed his eyes, but images of the hospital appeared behind his lids. Doctors and nurses in those funny pajama things. Lights so bright that all the shiny surfaces glistened. Mom in bed—pale, skinny, weak. A drugged smile when she saw him that didn't hide the pain. He wanted to hug her, but there were tubes and cords in her arms. He could only stand there and stare.

His eyes snapped open.

The ghost of disinfectant haunted his nasal cavity. He wondered if he would ever stop smelling that.

A slight roar came from outside. Danny jumped out of bed and dashed to the window, speckled with drops of water. He pressed his face against the glass and cupped his hands around his eyes to peer through the rivulets that distorted the view of the driveway. Puddles grew in the spot reserved for his mother's car.

She'll be home soon, he told himself. He recognized the tone as the same that Mom used when she said she wouldn't be out late, but would return after he was asleep. Another voice wormed its way into his mind—one that said, *It's raining. The roads are slick. She still doesn't have all her strength back.*

Danny pushed that aside. He was being a child. He was better than that. Everyone agreed how much of a big boy he was, how he could handle things. How proud they were that he could look after his sister and brother while his mom was away. How mature he was.

Even Mom said she didn't have to worry about him. She was more concerned about his younger siblings, especially Sam, who was traumatized by their mother's hospitalization.

"How could he understand? He's just a little kid!" Danny said to an empty room when he was certain he was alone. He dared not say it to any of the grownups. After all, he hard a hard time understanding it himself.

No one actually told him what was wrong with Mom. Was it cancer? He knew about cancer. His friend's grandpa died of that disease. A second grader in his school had leukemia, but Danny didn't believe that's what Mom had. Something with her stomach, he thought he heard someone say.

The important thing is she beat it. She came home from the hospital. She's better.

Well, maybe not perfect. She tired out easily and ate little. She became snappy at inconsequential things. However, Danny admired his mother for being determined—if she set her mind to do something, by gosh, she did it. That included going back to school.

Headlights cut through the rain, now a downpour. Danny's heart beat quickly. A vehicle approached the driveway…and then continued on past. He let out a huge, disappointed sigh.

He paced, cutting circles on the floorboards.

She had an accident. Her car is in a ditch somewhere. It slid on the wet road and she hit her head on the steering wheel and no one knows where she is and she's dying. Maybe already dead.

Tears burned his eyes.

Stop it! She's okay. Just at school, that's all.

That nagging voice persisted. *She should've been home by now. She got lost in the rain and now she's in a wrecked car. Or thrown out of it and lying in a puddle. Wet and dying and all alone.*

Thunder boomed in the distance.

Danny turned to the window, his breath hitching. The houses across the street lit up momentarily with lightning.

He dove into bed and yanked the blanket up to cover half his face. His wide eyes stared at the window that was now dark. Invisible rain pelted it, making machine-gun *pluh pluh pluhs.*

Come home, come home, come home, he repeated silently. His hands trembled, causing the blanket to vibrate in his vision.

She's okay, the voice of reason told him. *There's nothing to worry about. Remember, you're the mature kid in the family.*

He forced himself to inhale a deep breath and let it out slowly. It was a calming way to breathe. Karate class taught him that, though he quit the class when Mom got sick and wasn't able to take him anymore.

A term that he recently learned drifted through his thoughts. One that he wished he had never heard.

Relapse.

What if she had a relapse? What if it—whatever *it* was—came back? If she got sick at school, she could have collapsed and had to be taken to the hospital in an ambulance. If she returned there, he might never see her again.

The drone of the rain subsided, and it was only then that he realized he was sobbing when he heard his own halting gasps. He wiped away tears. This was not how a big boy, the big brother, should act. Mom would be disappointed.

Crying tired him out. His eyes drooped. He willed them open, but they betrayed him.

The muffled roar of an engine brought Danny back to consciousness. He dashed to the window.

A car had pulled into the driveway. Mom's car. The headlights turned off, then the driver's side door opened. His mother stepped out and opened an umbrella, although the rain was currently a light shower. She soon disappeared from his view, and he heard the front door open.

Danny crawled back into bed and snuggled into the blanket.

Mom was home. She was safe. Of course she was. Why would Danny think otherwise?

He drifted off to sleep and dreamed of hospitals.

"Where's the copier?" Ralph Kingsley asked the librarian.

The nameplate on the desk identified her as Cora Weston, but Ralph didn't care about her name. She was in her sixties with cat-eye glasses resting on the tip of her nose, and dawdled with another woman Ralph assessed at being a hundred and two. Cora ignored Ralph and continued to help the elderly lady.

Ralph impatiently nudged his way in front of the geezer and repeated, "Where's the copier?" He was late for an appointment with a client and he required copies made of important documents. In his haste, he only printed one copy of the contract and needed three originals. He didn't have time to drive back to his office to print more. And he certainly could not be held up in the library by a couple of old biddies.

The enormous woman behind the counter glared at Ralph. The glasses enlarged her eyes and gave them a hideous look. "Sir, you'll have to wait your turn."

"Lady, I need to use your copy machine. Now." He was

wasting time yapping with this hag. Clients had a way of leaving if you're late, and he couldn't afford to lose this one. Too much money was at stake.

"It's in the back, to the right," Cora snapped.

Ralph rushed from the desk and down an aisle of books.

"Oops, I forgot to tell him the machine has been acting strange all day," Cora said to the patron.

The grey-haired woman smiled. "It'll be a pity if it ruins whatever he has to copy."

Ralph deleted the librarian and her customer from his thoughts and focused on his imminent meeting with his client and the deal that would finally be sealed. For a while, he believed he could never convince that jerk to agree with his terms. His persuasive skills prevailed, and now only one step was left—the signing of the papers. In less than an hour, he'd have no more financial worries. He wished there were more suckers like this one in the world.

Reaching the far end of the library, he discovered the copy machine in a windowless corner. The fluorescent light above the beige boxy unit was unlit, so the copier hid in semi-darkness.

No, it wasn't hiding—it was lurking. Rather than cowering, it awaited an unsuspecting victim to come along, ready to pounce.

That's ridiculous, Ralph thought, and he shook his head to get rid of the crazy idea. *How could it be lurking? It's only a machine, for God's sake.*

Ralph took a deep breath and walked toward the copier, forcing himself to think about the client—and the money—he would lose if he didn't hurry.

The contraption made him uneasy. The lid was a giant, gaping mouth. A low, gurgling hum emanated from the machine.

Ralph opened the manila envelope he was carrying and pulled out a small stack of papers, his key to a gold mine. The machine was unequipped with an automatic feed, so he'd need to copy the document one page at a time. He placed the first one on the glass plate and lined it up with the guide markers, then lowered the lid gently, making sure not to disturb the placement of the paper.

How much did this thing cost, anyway? Everything was overpriced. To his surprise, a sign taped on the front of the copier proclaimed black and white letter-sized copies priced at ten cents. That's what he paid when he was a kid! Nothing stayed the same price. Ever.

He rooted in his pocket for change, which he always carried. The world's currency was becoming digital, but he insisted on actual hard cash. When the grid went down, he could still buy things.

His fingers detected a thin dime, which he retrieved and inserted it into the coin slot. He reached down to push the button marked PRINT, but retracted his hand. The button glowed an eerie green, like a jealous eye staring up at him with the word across drawn into the slit of a pupil, peering at him coldly.

He punched the button with his index finger, then drew his hand back and rubbed his eye.

The machine rumbled, and a bright light flashed from the sides of the lid. A sheet of paper slid out of a slot and rested on the plastic holder that jutted out like a square metal tail.

Ralph fetched the paper. It was a decent copy, except some words were slightly smeared. He adjusted the darkness, setting it to be lighter, and dropped a second dime in the coin slot. He pushed PRINT quickly.

The machine rumbled again, and light flashed from under the lid. It spewed out another page and became still.

Ralph examined that sheet. Now the words were almost illegible. He was certain turning down the darkness would make the copy clearer. He lifted the lid and looked at the original. Nothing wrong with it. He put it back in place and lowered the lid, then moved the lever completely to the LIGHT end.

His pocket contained no more dimes, but he found two nickels, which he fed to the machine. This time, he pushed PRINT hard and vicious.

The copier ejected another sheet, but this one only had black blobs and smears. Ralph crumpled the paper into a ball and furiously threw it on the floor. His hands shook as they always did when he became angry.

Ralph shifted the darkness lever all the way to the DARK end, then pulled out a handful of change. He inserted a quarter in the coin slot and slammed PRINT with his palm. The machine produced another copy, this one completely black.

Rage washed over Ralph, and he ripped the copy into tiny pieces and scattered them on the floor. Sweat rolled down his face, which turned a burning red. His suit stuck to his back, making him feel even hotter.

Ralph intended to storm to the front counter and tell that worthless librarian exactly what he thought of this broken-down machine, but remembered the copier should have given him change for his quarter. Despite the amount being insignificant, he wouldn't be ripped off any more.

He struck his index finger in the coin return cavity and felt around, but there were no coins, so he depressed the button for the coin return. Still, nothing came out. Losing his patience, Ralph balled up his fist and gave the side of the machine a couple of hard whacks and turned to march to the desk.

He had taken only three steps when the copier rumbled. The light shone under the lid. A sheet of paper shot out.

The stolen change must have caused the machine to make another copy. Except someone needed to push the PRINT button.

The machine thundered and shuddered again, and the interior light flashed once more. A sheet emerged from the bowels of the copier and landed on its predecessor. The copier continued this action, the light flashing repeatedly. More paper flew out, one page after another shot out faster and faster.

Returning to the copy machine, he didn't know what to think. The circuitry must be hosed, he thought. The wires are fried—that must be it.

He grabbed a sheet of paper as it emerged. Nothing but strange-looking blobs smeared across it. More papers shot out, and the smears were slightly different on each succeeding sheet. Incomprehensible patterns took shape by the sheets, landing rapidly on top of each other. An animated picture came to life right before Ralph's eyes that became more and more recognizable to him—familiar and frightening.

This bizarre cartoon unfolded before him, hypnotizing him. The figure became hideously clearer, and recognized the picture that was forming. He was staring down at his own portrait.

Ralph's heart seemed to stop. Paralysis squeezed him.

That's me! His mind screamed in terror. *That's me, oh my God, that's me. That repulsive thing is me!*

The pictures stopped coming out, and the light quit flashing. The machine became still and quiet except for the low rumbling deep down inside it.

Ralph gawked at this image, distorted and horrifying. He had to get out of here—run and keep running until he was far from this appalling picture and the monstrosity that could produce it. Despite the urge, he could not tear his eyes from it. The portrait stared back at him and grinned.

Finally, he twisted his head to the side and closed his eyes. After a moment, he grabbed his documents and rushed toward the exit. Then he remembered the paper under the lid. His impulse was to leave it and run, but he knew that without it, he could not sign the deal with his client.

Greed overcame instinct, terror forgotten.

He lifted the lid and let it bang against the wall, then reached down to grab the document. When his fingers touched it, the paper dissolved into the glass plate.

Shock and confusion gripped him. He felt around to check if it had slid into the machine somehow. He couldn't believe this—losing it meant surrendering his gold mine.

His fear evolved into rage. If the copier refusing to work right caused him to be late, he could call the client and say he was running a few minutes behind schedule. But the machine stealing an important page and causing him to lose his money was a different story.

He struck the glass with his open palm, then pounded it several more times, each time putting more force behind it. Each strike compounded his fury.

In his rage, Ralph did not hear the growl deep inside the copier growing stronger.

He stopped beating the glass and kicked the machine's hard shell, denting and cracking it.

The copier shook, as if becoming angry.

Ralph raised his fist over his head, then swung it down with all his strength. Something in his hand crunched, but the satisfaction of breaking the glass superseded the injury. A spiderweb of cracks spread. A thin smirk crossed his face.

The lid crashed down on his hand. He yelped and attempted to retrieve his trapped appendage, but it refused to budge. His hand howled. He pulled harder, trying to free it, to no avail. Searing pain shot up his arm to his shoulder.

Panic set in and he tried to pry the lid open, but it was clamped shut. His face twisted into a red, sweaty mask, replicating the picture that the copier had produced just a short time ago.

The machine convulsed violently. The light under the lid blared, momentarily obscuring Ralph's vision. His surroundings reappeared as a sheet of paper fell onto the tray. It was an image of his hand.

The blinding light blazed, and a jolt of pain shot up Ralph's arm. He shrieked and held onto the machine with his free hand to steady himself against the agony. Another page appeared, and the pain eased. This image was of a hand with missing fingers.

The copy machine roared, the horrible groan of the motor sounding like gnawing. He felt a tug on his arm, then an unknown force yanked his arm under the lid to the elbow. He cried out in anguish.

The next copy showed a severed arm.

Seeing this new copy, Ralph thrashed about, trying desperately to free himself. His arm felt like it was being torn off.

The light exploded once more, and his arm descended entirely under the lid.

Ralph screamed. Consciousness faded away, and he collapsed.

The unseen force continued pulling him into the machine. His head disappeared. The copy that slid out next was similar to the picture that had revolted him several minutes earlier.

The machine proceeded to produce copies until Ralph was entirely ingested, and then it settled into silence once more. The green PRINT button gleamed with contentment.

The librarian hurried to see what the commotion was all about. She had been on the phone when she heard the racket, but ignored it. However, when the man screamed, she hung up and rushed to investigate. It served that irritating man right if the copy machine was giving him problems, but she didn't want him to electrocute himself. The insurance claim would be a nightmare.

That man was nowhere in sight when she entered the nook containing the copier. Paper was strewn all over the floor. It looked like the machine had gone insane.

She sighed and gathered the sheets of paper until she noticed they were pictures of human parts—an arm, a leg, a foot. One was a picture of a face—that man's face.

She dropped the stack and instinctively backed up. Her stomach churned, and a thousand ideas of what had happened crossed her mind at once, but she dismissed them all as lunacy. She regarded the copier.

The librarian trembled involuntarily. For some morbid reason, she had an irresistible urge to see what was under the lid. The few feet she had to cross stretched out for a mile. Upon reaching the copier, she slowly lifted the lid. The glass plate was shattered, but pieces were still intact.

Her image reflected up at her from a thousand tiny surfaces, which gave her apprehension so powerful, she dropped the lid. Without thinking, she quickly reached behind the copier, unplugged it, and ran back to her office. She was now sick to her stomach, so she closed the library and drove home. Tomorrow, she would call someone to take the machine away. She would NOT order another copier.

The copy machine sat silently in its corner, resting in its cold sleep. The building was dim, with the only illumination streaming through the slits in the Venetian blinds. That was okay. The copier didn't need light—it could make its own.

The plug lay on the floor with the cord coiled in several loops. Almost imperceptibly, it slithered across the floor and to the base of the wall, where it climbed upward to the electric socket and plugged itself in.

The motor inside the copier whirred as electricity powered it. The green PRINT button lit up.

The copy machine waited patiently in the dimly lit library amid the wealth of knowledge. It had information of its own and people would need its services. It would happily oblige.

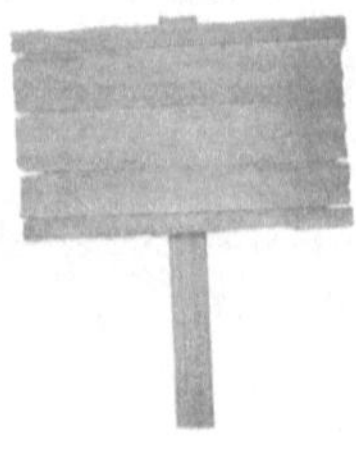

Michael Harper sipped his coffee while walking across campus, willing the caffeine to energize him. It wasn't working. He passed by the high school students gathering in the courtyard prior to class starting, but they barely registered to him. Just bodies taking up space, wanting to be there no more than he did. They would soon be gone—unlike him.

How many years had he dedicated to this school? Eighteen? Nineteen? Did it matter? The school system allowed teachers to retire after twenty-five years, but now the politicians running education who had not stepped foot inside a school since they themselves graduated were considering increasing it to thirty. Why not? Who cared? It's not like he had any plans after being released from his servitude, anyway.

Once in his classroom, Michael checked his email. No surprises—administrators letting the faculty know about a pep rally that afternoon, because disrupting class was less important than showing school spirit to budding athletes; parents asking why their precious darlings were failing despite them having access to an online portal that showed every assignment and their corresponding grades; students begging for extra credit after refusing to complete the actual work; and other teachers sharing gallows humor to cut through the bleakness of their profession.

First period arrived. Like him, most of the students hadn't yet awoken. That would change by second period, when he would be unable to quiet them down for the initial five minutes of class—if at all.

Freshmen.

What made him think he would impact the lives of this gaggle of fourteen- and fifteen-year-olds? Year after year, he saw the same types enter and exit. After a while, they all blended together. Sure, a few stood out among the sea of pimples and attitude, but by year's end, they moved on to other teachers to be replaced by a new crop of adolescents. He'd forget their names ten months later, and they would certainly forget him.

When Michael was a student himself, he dreamed of being a writer. He wanted to change the world with his words. He thought he could positively affect others. Reality set in during college and he realized that his best prospect for a job would be to teach English, so he switched his major to education with a minor in literature. His first several years of teaching were exciting as he tried to connect to the youth under his charge. But years of bureaucracy, apathy, and outright hostility toward his chosen profession wore him down like constant rain eroding a mountain.

He had to get through one more day. Then another after that.

Next week, he'd be introducing his ninth graders to *Romeo and Juliet*. He used to love Shakespeare, but he could only hear the halting recitals from adolescents struggling to form their mouths around the Bard's words so many times before he wanted to burn down the Globe. For now, he was pushing them through a unit on poetry to prime them for Willy Shakes's iambic pentameter.

Michael lucked out this year as fourth period—his planning time—was right after lunch, so he ended up with an hour and a half reprieve from the madness of teenagers. It broke the day up nicely and allowed him to focus on grading papers, a chore he did quickly and, he hated to admit, somewhat carelessly. Once upon a time, he spent hours after school immersed in correcting every grammatical error on essays and providing critical feedback to assist in the maturity of his students in their grasp of the English language. Eventually, he realized that was futile, as the kids didn't care. Why should he?

Fifth period arrived. Home stretch, considering the sixth and final period of the day would be interrupted by the *rah-rah-go-team* assembly in the gymnasium. He had all his classes working on a free verse poem. He might have sixth period write it for homework or maybe just forgo the assignment altogether. That would be easier on him.

He wandered up and down the aisles, refocusing students back on task despite how desperately they disliked writing. You'd think creating a poem was equivalent to being waterboarded.

"Mr. Harper?" a timid voice said. It belonged to a girl named Jasmine who rarely spoke in class. If he called on her, she would slink down in her seat and mutter mostly one-word answers. She clutched a sheet of notebook paper as if it were a top secret correspondence.

"What do you need?"

"Well, I…um…I'm done."

"Okay, put it in the basket."

"I was…well, could you, you know…read it?" She was close to hyperventilating.

"Sure." Michael took the paper from her and retreated to his desk in the front corner of the room.

Jasmine slinked away to her desk near the back, but kept her eyes locked on him. She bit her upper lip.

The poem was short:

THE VOID by Jasmine Tyson

I stand at the void
The deep nothingness draws me in
I stare
It calls
I want to step into it
The blackness surrounds me, comforts me
I am afraid
What if I go?
I want to go
I don't want to go
The void is all
There is nothing left

Michael found his hands shaking. He took a deep breath. Then another. He looked out at the classroom, unaware that half the students were already talking to each other, since his attention was elsewhere. He met Jasmine's eyes, which were wide and nervous, then waved at her to beckon her to him.

With shoulders hunched, Jasmine inched her way to his desk. Now she did not meet his gaze, but stared at the floor.

"Jasmine, this is very powerful."

Her eyes flicked up at him, but only for a moment. "You think so?"

"Yes." He forced a swallow down his throat. "D-do you feel like this?"

Her voice was a mere squeak. "Sometimes."

"A lot?"

She didn't respond right away, but finally nodded.

Michael exhaled. The class grew talkative, but that was acceptable. Their noise was a shelter. "I'm going to ask you a question. You don't have to answer if you don't want to. Okay?"

Jasmine's head bobbed up and down a fraction of an inch, enough to be a positive response.

"Do you ever feel like you want to end it all?"

Jasmine lifted her eyes to meet his. This time for a long moment. Tears welled up. "Sometimes."

"Do you have anyone to talk to? Your parents? Friends? A pastor?"

She shook her head. Tears now flowed down her cheek.

Michael leaned in close to her. The din of the class was

white noise in the background. "Listen to me. You don't have to be alone. I will get you help. Okay?"

An expression crossed Jasmine's face that was a mixture of anguish, fear, and relief.

Michael knew not to touch a student. It would take one kid in the classroom to snap a cellphone photo and he'd be in hot water—but he didn't care. He gently clasped one of her hands in both of his. She needed comfort, and this was the least he could provide. "You'll get through this. You'll be okay."

She nodded again, more vigorously than before, and then wiped her eyes with the back of her hand. He found a tissue and gave it to her.

"Why don't you go to the bathroom and freshen up," he said.

She hurried out of the room.

The other students were engaged in their own conversations, oblivious to what transpired at the teacher's desk. A few minutes later, Jasmine returned, face washed, and reclaimed her seat as if nothing had happened. Michael allowed the class free time for the rest of the period. He had other things on his mind. When the bell rang and the students dashed from the room, Jasmine trailed behind. Before she walked through the door, she flashed Michael a quick smile.

Michael delivered his sixth period class to the gym so they could be filled with pep. Teachers were supposed to supervise, but mostly they stood along the wall talking to each other while the athletes made a show of themselves and the kids in the bleachers cheered. However, more important things required his attention.

He met with the guidance counselor and debriefed her. The counselor would notify a social worker to register Jasmine in a program to work through her problems. There were no guarantees, but the girl would receive help.

And he would monitor her situation, at least until the end of the school year. Maybe longer.

Michael climbed into his car after the students cleared off campus and thought he might do this job for a few more years.

"The store closes in ten minutes," a pleasant voice over the intercom said. "Please make your final purchases now."

Margaret looked for her son. As usual, Jimmy was nowhere in sight. The six-year-old was probably running around somewhere or looking at toys. She could never keep track of him when she took him shopping.

She dropped the can of spaghetti sauce into the buggy, then resumed pushing the metal contraption with the broken front wheel down the aisle. She had more items she wanted to buy, but they would have to wait until tomorrow. Right now, she had to find Jimmy.

Margaret rounded the corner and headed down the long row at the rear of the store and past the meat section. Other shoppers passed her as they made their way toward the cashiers. She glanced down each aisle, but her son was nowhere to be found. She would locate him with the toys at the far end. It astonished her how someone so young could sneak away with such dexterity.

Her pace increased. A fishy odor wafted past her from the meat department.

Shopping this close to closing time made her nervous. She usually planned her visit for earlier in the day, but she was late leaving the office. Work piled up and had to be finished. When she picked up Jimmy, the babysitter hassled her about being paid early. Margaret told her she didn't have the money and would have to wait until payday. The babysitter begged for at least a partial payment, so Margaret gave her the last bit of cash in her purse to shut her up. She debated skipping shopping today, but there were so many things that she needed...

Finally, Margaret reached the toy aisle and turned the corner. "Jim—"

The aisle was empty.

Great, just great, she thought. Jimmy, don't do this to me.

Her brain worked fast. The store carried a few aquariums, and her son enjoyed watching the fish.

She rushed to a nook behind a collection of plants where the fish tanks were located.

There's no such thing as grocery stores anymore, she thought. *They're more like flea markets.*

She exhaled a deep breath in relief when she saw a familiar tow-head needing a haircut tapping on a container's glass to get the fish's attention.

"Jimmy! There you are."

"Mommy!" Jimmy said with a big smile as he looked up at her. She picked him up and set him in the child seat in the buggy. She always kept the spot clear of groceries in case he grew tired of walking.

"Don't disappear like that," Margaret scolding him calmly as she pushed the cart toward the cash registers. "You scared Mommy. You don't want to be locked in, do you?"

"No," his little voice said.

"You will, if you keep wandering off." *Just like your father wandered off.*

"Are we going home now?" Jimmy asked. He was the spitting image of his dad, with his white-blonde hair and grey eyes that could melt a glacier. Sometimes, when Margaret looked at her son, Dale's memory would invade her mind. For months after he left, she missed him so much that she was in physical distress and didn't know how she could live without him. Eventually, the pain dissipated, replaced with anger and hatred for what he did to her. For what he did to Jimmy.

"The store will close in five minutes," the voice over the intercom said. It was more abrupt than the last announcement and brought Margaret back to reality.

Just enough time to buy this stuff and get out of here, she thought and lined up behind a harried-looking middle-aged woman unloading her own groceries.

"Want to help me unload the buggy?" Margaret asked Jimmy when a spot cleared on the conveyor belt at the register.

Jimmy shook his head "no," and his upper torso pivoted back and forth in his over-emphasis so he looked similar to a cartoon character. "I want *down.*"

"All right, but stay right here." She hurriedly lifted him from the buggy and set him next to it. She hastily unloaded her groceries as he turned his attention to the candy display.

The cashier ran each item over the price scanner at her own slow pace. Painfully aware of the time, Margaret silently urged her to move faster. Finally, the cashier told her the total. As she put her credit card in the reader, she glanced down to check on the boy.

He was gone once again.

She clenched her fists to keep her hands from shaking and turned away from the cashier. "Jimmy? *Jimmy!*"

"You now have two minutes," the intercom voice said with no pleasantness left in it.

Margaret rushed away from the register, leaving her card dangling from the reader.

Her son was nowhere in sight.

"Come here! Now!" She didn't wait to see if he came out of hiding. He liked to play hide and seek.

One customer in a small group filing out the automatic doors spared a sympathetic glance at Margaret as she raced down the rows of empty check-out lines, calling her son's name.

Panic grew inside her. The windows at the front of the store displayed the last of the shoppers heading toward their cars in the mostly vacant parking lot. No sign of a small boy, Jimmy must have still been in the building.

Margaret dashed to the aquariums, praying he was there. She held her breath as she passed the plants (*ridiculous selling plants in a grocery store!*). The nook was void of people. Fish swam placidly in their watery universes, oblivious to her or anything else.

The overhead lights dimmed, then came on again—a signal the store was ready to close.

Something caught her eye, and she strained her neck muscles, turning her head. At the far end of the aisle, Jimmy disappeared behind an end-cap display. His giggling was faint, but distinct.

"James Michael Willingham!" she yelled. When she called him that, she meant business. Time was running short, so she bolted away from the plants (*stupid plants*).

"Thirty seconds before doors are locked."

Come on feet, go a little faster, she pleaded, ignoring her screaming appendages. She desperately wanted to kick off her shoes. While she had never been athletic, she now felt every pound she had gained over the last few years.

Sliding around a display of potato chips, Margaret almost slammed into the shelves.

Jimmy stood half-way down the aisle, looking at cereal boxes. Like the fish, he was oblivious to her.

"Jimmy!" she yelled in anguish.

The boy's head jerked up, startled. The sight of her amused him—he gave her a malicious grin, then shot off elsewhere.

Terror gripped Margaret. She raced after him, pushing herself to her limit. Her overworked lungs clawed in her chest, causing her to gasp for breath. Having no voice, she could not yell at him anymore.

Jimmy reached the end of the aisle and turned the *wrong* direction, away from the exit.

Margaret grasped for him. Her fingers grazed the fabric of his shirt. She seized it as if her life depended on it.

The next moment, she had the boy's arm and swept him up in the air.

The lights flashed once again. On, off, on, off.

Margaret spun toward the exit.

All customers had fled. With registers closed, the cashiers marched to the office. The automatic doors were still open.

Margaret's husband had run out on her. Now she was doing the running, running to save her son, the only one left in her life. The only person who mattered.

She sprinted past the counters. Only a few more yards to go.

A stark door opened. Several men wearing black hooded jackets stepped out, armed with high-powered rifles.

A laugh of despair escaped Margaret.

Adults often threatened their children with the grocery militia to scare them into behaving—*she* had done it herself to Jimmy, but he was too young to fully comprehend.

The glass door before her slid on its track, about to shut.

"No!"

The militia shouldered their weapons and took aim.

In desperation, she threw Jimmy toward the closing door. He flew through the diminishing clearance and tumbled to the cement outside.

The lights turned off.

The door had mere few inches to go. Too narrow for Margaret to fit through. Regardless, she slammed into the glass and pushed, using all her strength to force the door open again.

A high-pitched electronic alarm blared.

"The store is now closed."

Margaret screamed.

The door moved slightly.

Guns fired.

All went black. When her sight returned, Margaret lay on the sidewalk outside the store.

The glass door snapped shut with small chips in the bulletproof glass where the rounds had struck, having barely missed her.

Jimmy's tiny arm clung to her, and she pulled him into a tight hug.

"Oh, Mommy, Mommy..."

"It's all right," she whispered. She never wanted to let him go. "We're safe now."

She was alive with her son. Nothing else mattered—not work, not the babysitter, and not even Dale.

Just her and Jimmy.

Mr. Wegner gave a cursory glance at the next referral. As Dean of Students at Cross Creek Middle School, he was the administrator kids saw when they got in trouble. Though still receiving teacher's pay, this position was the first step for him to move up the ladder and eventually be in charge of his own school. He had merely been at this job for half of the fall semester, and already the grind of dealing out daily discipline took its toll on him. He enjoyed engaging with kids, not punishing them.

Another case of bullying. Of course. No matter how many anti-bullying signs they hung, how often counselors lectured, how often teachers trained to identify and handle the situation, it still happened. Certain kids were hard-wired to be horrible to those weaker than themselves. Initially, he treated cases like this with patience and care, demonstrating empathy and attempting to teach the bully to recognize and change the inappropriate behavior. Now, he meted swift justice.

Details on the referral were sparse, but two seventh-grade boys were involved. In the gym locker room, Caleb Jackson stole Galen Bartholomew's clothes, leaving the victim in his underwear, called him unfortunate names, and pushed him to the floor. The P.E. coach heard the name calling and witnessed the physical assault, and then found Galen's clothes wadded up in a trash can.

He opened his office door to greet the parties sitting in the waiting room. Typical of boys that age, the two had a striking difference. One was massive for a 12-year-old with a scowl and inset eyes. Wegner recognized this brute as one of the football players. The other boy was half the size of the linebacker—short, skinny, and wearing glasses too large for his narrow, pointy face. The Hulk T-shirt he wore evidently reflected his feelings of being meek Bruce Banner raging at those bigger, stronger, and meaner than himself.

Wegner pointed at the larger one. "You. In here. Now." The kid stood up and shambled into the office. He was nearly as tall as the Dean, even with his head bowed. To the tiny boy, Wegner said in a softer voice, "I'll talk to you in a few minutes. Just sit tight."

The door slammed harder than Wegner intended. It was unprofessional to allow his emotions to overwhelm him, but he was sick of seeing the abuse of power. The bully plopped in the guest chair, and Wegner loomed over him for a long, painful moment. Let him feel what it's like for someone larger to intimidate him for a change. Finally, Wegner sat.

"What were you thinking? Do you enjoy being mean to other kids? Is that it?"

"No, I..."

"Do you have any idea what he went through?" Wegner pointed at the door. The volume of his voice raised a notch. Maybe two notches. "Just because you're twice his size doesn't give you the right to do what you did. You think it's a joke, but taking someone's clothes and humiliating them is not acceptable. For theft alone, I can instruct the resource officer to take you away in handcuffs. And you *dared* lay your hands on him? Not only are you looking at suspension, but being sent to an alternative school. Do you know the kinds of kids who go there?"

The boy's lower lip quivered. "But…"

"And that's only if his parents don't press charges. Then you're facing jail time."

Tears welled up in the kid's eyes and streamed down his cheeks.

"Not so tough now, are you, Caleb?"

"I'm not Caleb."

"Wait…what?"

The boy's voice hitched. "I'm Galen."

"Have your I.D. on you?"

The crying boy rooted in his pocket and then pulled out a plastic card that showed a photo of him with the name "Galen Bartholomew" and a student number printed on it.

Wegner felt like crawling under his desk. "Um…tell me what happened in the locker room."

Galen wiped his face with his meaty fingers. "I was changing out of my P.E. clothes and Caleb grabbed them all and laughed at me and ran away. I told him to give them back, but he just kept calling me GAY-len BARFolomew, then threw them in the garbage. I tried to take them out, and when I bent over, he pushed me from behind and I fell to the floor." He sniffed, and then blurted, "He does this to me ALL THE TIME!"

Wegner reached across his desk and placed a hand on Galen's shoulder. "I'm very sorry I got you confused. I just assumed…you're so much bigger than him. Why do you let him pick on you?"

Galen looked at the Dean with a mixture of confusion and horror. "I don't *hurt* people. You think because I'm big, I should be like that? I *hate* violence."

"Aren't you a football player?"

Galen's expression became one of someone speaking to a stupid person. "I *block* other players. Who are my size. And padded! I don't beat them up. It's a game. You know, for fun."

Wegner found his fingernails very interesting.

"Am I still in trouble?"

"No, of course not. Gather your things and go back to class."

Galen stood and headed out.

"Oh, and Galen," Wegner said. "I'm sorry. I'll make sure Caleb stops harassing you."

After Galen exited, Wegner crooked his finger at the remaining student, motioning for him to join him.

They both sat, and Wegner regarded the slight boy sitting across from him. Caleb showed no remorse and no fear. Only a blank expression.

"Tell me what happened."

Caleb shrugged.

"I said tell me."

"It was a joke. Sheesh, no one has a sense of humor."

"I understand you keep targeting Galen."

Caleb snorted.

"What's so funny?"

"Nothing." Yet he still smirked.

"I'm getting a little tired of your attitude."

Behind the oversized glasses, Caleb's eyes rolled.

Wegner took a deep breath to calm himself. "I just want to know one thing. Why?"

One of Caleb's scrawny shoulders raised in a half-shrug. "Why not?"

Anson phased in and realized he was not where he intended to go. The heat hit him first—his skin's nerve endings were more sensitive than the rest of his sensory organs.

The dark gray of his vision burst into bright blindness and he threw his hands over his eyes to block out the intensity. Slowly, he peeked through his fingers, squinting against the glare. As his eyesight adjusted, his new surroundings came into focus.

A vast canyon sprawled before him. Trees that looked like twigs stretched up from the depth of the gigantic ravine. A sliver of a stream that was certainly a raging river scratched its way through fuzzy foliage. Anson stood on the precipice—if he had phased in a third of a meter forward, he would have appeared mid-air and subsequently fallen to his death.

Stupid! he silently scolded himself. *Gotta be more careful.*

He crept back from the ledge, and dirt crumbled from the spot his toes vacated. His heart's beat thrummed in his chest as full understanding hit him how close to fatal this trip nearly was. His legs turned wobbly and his knees folded. He plopped to the ground, trembling.

After drawing several shaky breaths, Anson regained control of his mutinous body. "Okay, where am I?" he asked, his voice a mere croak. It had been at least a year since his vocal cords had finally stopped betraying him when he spoke, and he disliked the raspy sound they now made, even if no one was in the vicinity to hear it.

He jumped to his feet and spun around. Yep, that confirmed it—absolutely no human was near, possibly for kilometers. Maybe longer.

Okay, concentrate. Concentrate. Concentrate. He concentrated.

His destination was Paris, so how did he end up here? Wherever here was. He missed the mark before—he was still learning how to phase. Just never this far. He definitely was *not* in Paris.

He ran through his lessons on phasing. Focus your mind on your destination. *Check.* Enter a meditative state. *Check.* Allow your body to become transcorporeal. *Check.* Tap into the photonic stream. *Check.* Create a psychic sight-line to your target location. *Check.* Launch yourself into the phase stream. *Double check.*

So where did he go wrong?

Anson always had problems with this part, causing both him and his Mentor much grief. It was rare that he would end up exactly where he wished to go, though usually he arrived just a few meters away from his target. He always tried to land in an open field because he heard stories of people phasing into walls or moving vehicles— and here he nearly ended up a cautionary tale himself. If he had gone into the canyon, would anyone have been able to trace him there to retrieve his body?

The thought of plummeting through the air caused Anson to shudder. He wondered morbidly if he would have felt the impact upon hitting the ground.

Stop it, stupid. Can't think of that. Gotta figure out where I am.

The problem with phasing was it depended on your knowledge of your destination—not with your mind, but with your body. You had to feel part of the geography. The photonic stream operated like air currents because it flowed in a specific course that countless factors could alter.

Something sparked in Anson's recollection. The photonic stream. The flow. Was the current disrupted?

Disequilibrium threatened him. A ghost of a memory nagged at him. He remembered the moment he phased out. Preternatural calm swept through his muscles as his consciousness dove into the stream. And then...and then...

Much like a mirage on a distant plain, a wavering occurred. A slight distortion. But in his noncorporeal condition, with his mind in flux, his whole existence distorted. And while the entire phasing process was nontraumatic, awareness rocketed into a *heightened plane*, like the most vivid dream imaginable. Once the phasing reached its conclusion, the trip evaporated into forgetfulness like a reflection of a setting sun on water.

Anson tried to force his brain to remember other trips he took where he missed his destination. Did he also experience those disruptions? He wanted to believe that he did, but was unconvinced those memories were real.

A more disturbing idea crept into his thoughts—if this happened to him, how many other people encountered it? And why didn't the Mentors know about it? If they were aware of the distortions, wouldn't they warn their students and tell them how to overcome it?

Unless it was impossible to overcome.

By not warning their students, they'd be responsible for accidents that occurred—and any deaths caused by those accidents.

Like his near death.

"Let's say that distortion threw me off track and sent me here," Anson said, his voice coming out less crackly now. He paced in a circle, as he did when he was deep in thought. "All I have to do is pay attention to it and avoid it. Then I'll get to where I'm going. Right. It's gotta work that way." He hoped.

He cautiously returned to the edge of the cliff and peered at the great expanse. Was this the Grand Canyon? He wasn't aware of other geographic formations like this, though it was possible.

We'll go with the Grand Canyon for now, he told himself.

He stepped away from the cliff. No sense tempting fate.

Anson prepped himself for the phase. The calming period took him about a quarter of an hour. He focused his mind on Paris. All else fell from his consciousness. His breathing and heart rate slowed to a minimum. He detected the molecules in his body separate from their solid stage—this part was always the most unsettling to him, so it required more effort to maintain the meditation.

As his physical form became insubstantial, his mental state transitioned from its usual existence into that of energy. The photonic stream flowed about him. He didn't see it with his eyes, as his body ceased ordinary functions —instead, he sensed the packets of light swirl around him. Once there, he projected his mind out, thinking *PARIS!*

Time in the photon stream was difficult to calculate and was malleable. And with his extreme awareness, his perception of time distorted. Eternity and an instant wove together into a concept the human brain couldn't decipher. The image of the familiar city materialized. He searched through the old-fashioned streets and ancient buildings until his essence located a park under the ruins of the Eiffel Tower. He directed his total attention to it.

Wait! The distortion!

He had nearly forgotten about it. If he somehow caused the distortion, then he needed to find out why. Or at the very least, identify it.

Anson widened his perception and tapped into the photon stream. He forced himself to go even deeper into the energy around and through him.

There it was—that ripple, starting like an echo in the distance, then rolling toward him. It was tough to reach out his senses around him and continue to link the image of Paris, especially when the distortion hit. The impact reeled him, and he struggled to maintain control. He rode it out.

As soon as the distortion passed, he launched himself.

A cool breeze played over his bare arms and face. The

light wasn't as painfully bright as his last phase-in, but it still took a few seconds for his eyes to adjust. Finally, he opened them and gazed up at the steel A-framed construction. The top part of the tower had collapsed before Anson was born.

He was exactly where he meant to be.

Now he had to find his Parisian Mentor. And discuss his discovery.

Anson wondered, *What will he say?*

Austin froze in place. An odd sensation ran through his torso, hot and cold at the same time. His breathing increased, threatening to hyperventilate.

No, it can't be him.

His legs moved of their own volition, edging toward the man Austin was sure was his former business partner —his former friend—yet equally convinced it couldn't be.

The man's hair was longer, curling into tangles. Austin even thought he caught glimpses of gray strands woven into the mop. But that profile was unmistakable, though was now on the pudgy side. Same with that carefree slouch that screamed, "I'm harmless, just a regular ol' fun-loving dude. You can *trust* me!"

Austin's fingers balled into a tight fist. He abhorred violence, but the one instance he nearly fell victim to its call was the last time he saw Chuck Witherspoon. He fought the urge to punch that smug, arrogant face to a bloody pulp. His intense anger brought him to the brink of the loss of self-control, and it terrified him.

And now, after five years, that same fury boiled inside him again.

Thirty feet away. Twenty-five feet. The crowd in the lobby of the convention center faded from view as his focus zeroed in on Chuck. Austin was certain it was him. It couldn't be an error.

Sweat rolled into Austin's eyes.

Twenty.

How the hell did he end up here? Austin's mind swirled. The last time he saw Chuck Witherspoon was in Tampa, and six months later, Austin packed up his few belongings to move to Indianapolis to start fresh. New job, new opportunity. Forget the old life and his shattered dreams.

They had been college buddies, both of them studying computer programming. Austin minored in art with a plan to go into app design, which he excelled at. Chuck had little interest in learning the skills to be proficient at anything technical or artistic. However, he had charisma and could charm the pants off anyone—which Austin discovered was not just an expression. Chuck could get any girl he wanted, and arranged Austin with numerous women over the years as well. This was definitely a perk, because Austin's self-esteem largely prevented him from pursuing the opposite sex.

Then came the proposition.

"Form a company?" The thought intimidated Austin.

"We're the perfect team," Chuck explained. "You handle the app design. I take care of business. We put in sweat equity and investors will pay for the startup."

Austin figured if anyone could convince investors to put up money on a couple of recent graduates, it would be

Chuck. They made a deal—on a handshake. What's a contract between friends?

He set to work, filing through one idea after another. Finally, the two decided on the concept of an app that assisted the average person through daily life. The app was more than a to-do list and more than a planner—it would allow people to manage every aspect of their daily interactions with a fun, easy-to-use interface. Success was surefire.

Except the investment never came. Promises, yes. Money, no.

"We need to put up a grand apiece. That's it."

"I thought we were putting in sweat equity," Austin said, irritated because two years had gone by and Chuck's promises had been unfruitful. Austin was working a job just to make ends meet while spending every evening coding his future.

"Trust me on this. If we put up our own money, it'll show investors we're serious."

The thousand dollars turned into two. Then five. And ten. Austin lost count, as a good portion of his paycheck went into expenses that Chuck promised were warranted.

One night, Austin was at a friend's house watching a football game and met a guy named Robert, who was an accountant. Austin shared with him his story, and Robert got concerned. "Let me look at your finances."

With effort since he was terrible at keeping track of money, Austin pulled together receipts, bank statements, and anything else he could regarding the financials of the company he shared with Chuck. After about a week,

Robert gave him the obvious bad news—Chuck had scammed him.

Austin confronted Chuck, still not completely convinced that his buddy had ripped him off.

"What did you do with the money?" Austin could barely get the words out.

"What do you mean?"

"All the money I gave you."

"I told you what I did with it. Calm down."

"Don't tell me to calm down! Did you put in any money?"

"Of course."

"Not according to my accountant."

Chuck blew air between clenched teeth. "You went to an accountant? You didn't trust me? Man, that hurts."

"Don't make yourself into a victim. You *stole* my money! Did you have any intention to actually getting investors?"

"Of course. But it takes money to make money."

"MY money!"

Chuck flashed him his award-winning smile. Friendly, comforting, assuring. "We're partners. I wouldn't let you down."

For a moment, Austin almost believed him.

"You used me. I built the app. Me. And then you took my money. I'm broke because of your promises. Your *lies*."

"Austin, don't be like this."

"Why did you lie to me?"

Chuck's smile faltered. An expression Austin wasn't used to seeing on Chuck's face appeared—open honesty. "I had to."

Austin exploded inside. Fortunately for both of them, the explosion stayed internal, otherwise Austin would have ended up in jail and Chuck in the hospital, or worse. Later, he had no memory of what he said to Chuck, and in a way, he was grateful.

That ended his dream of being successful with his own company and creation. He immediately flooded his resume to drown prospective employers with his qualifications. A software company in Indianapolis threw him a lifeline.

Now, five years later, that all seemed like a dream. It took two years for his anger at Chuck to abate, though that burning rage still crawled out of hiding now and then. Fortunately, life moved on, as it had a tendency to do.

Austin never expected to see Chuck again. Yet now his former business partner stood before him.

Ten feet.

Chuck—Austin now had no doubt it actually was Chuck—engaged in conversation with a pretty young woman. His next mark, no doubt.

Five.

Chuck's voice penetrated the din of the crowd. "Upstairs? Where's the stairs?"

"Down the hall. You can't miss them. There's an escalator, too." The woman sounded slightly irritated.

"Oh, I like escalators."

The woman delivered a patronizing smile, then disappeared from Austin's vision.

Austin fought the urge to smash his fist against the

back of Chuck's head, but tapped him on the shoulder instead. Chuck turned to him and smiled.

Anger dissipated like steam, leaving behind confusion.

Chuck's smile was slack, not sly. His eyes were vacant, with no recognition of Austin in them.

"Chuck? Chuch Witherspoon?"

"Yeah. That's me. Chuck." His smile widened, but his eyes remained blank.

Austin examined his former friend. He looked a decade older. He had put on weight and subtle lines etched his doughy face.

"It's me. Austin Naughton."

As if in slow motion, realization seeped into Chuck's expression. "Oh *yeah!* Austin!" He embraced Austin with a tight grip.

Austin pulled away. Chuck smiled at him, but didn't say a word. It was a radiant smile, very different from Chuck's patented inauthentic grin he used to con people. It reminded Austin of a three-year-old at the zoo for the first time, as if everything was new and exciting for Chuck. Yet, his eyes showed a vacantness as well, like his comprehension wasn't clicking.

What's wrong with him? Austin stepped back and stared at Chuck, who was no longer Chuck. Had he been in an accident? An illness? Did he scam the wrong person who didn't hold back?

"H-how are you?" Austin asked.

"I'm good. I'm working a booth. We're selling..." He furrowed his brow. "Stuff. But I'm lost. It's upstairs."

Intense sadness poured through Austin. Hatred at

Chuck at ate him over the last few years, but seeing him now was worse. He choked back tears.

"Come on. I'll show you where the stairs are."

Barry slid his arms into his padded winter coat, even though the calendar said it was still autumn. He had finished dinner and had to feed the horses, his primary chore now that he was ten. When he assumed that responsibility, he swelled with the pride of maturity, which all too soon passed into the tedium of drudgery. Whining did no good—he was told, "They don't eat, you don't eat." It was best just to do it without talking back, otherwise there were consequences.

It wasn't hard. In the morning, throw a chunk of hay into the pasture and fill their trough with water, then give them a bucket of grain in the evening. Since the Daylight Savings time change occurred, the nightly feedings now took place after dark.

He located the silver flashlight, but it didn't turn on when he tested it. "Dad, the flashlight doesn't work."

"Put new batteries in it," his father said. He was stretched out on his recliner in the family room, and his voice rose over a sitcom laugh track emanating from the TV. He chugged from the bottle.

Barry dug in the junk drawer in the kitchen and found one nine-volt and a AA. However, the flashlight took C-cells. "We ain't got none!"

"Don't say 'ain't'. Makes you sound like an ijit." The sitcom audience laughed, as if on cue.

The boy located two more flashlights, neither of which worked.

Nothing ever works around here, Barry thought.

He turned on the floodlight outside the sliding glass door. It lit up the backyard, but it didn't throw far enough to reach the barn.

Barry stepped into the garage and slipped on his sneakers that were stiff from the cold. He had to re-tie the left shoe because it was too loose. For reasons he never figured out, that shoe always became untied.

"Close the damn door! You're letting in the co—"

THMMP!

The wooden door pulled shut and cut off his dad's words. The large carport door vibrated against with wind, the metallic din reverberating off the cement floor and bare walls.

Barry sighed. *Gotta get this over with. Flashlight or no flashlight.*

As he stepped outside, a frigid blast struck him. He wondered how it got so cold so fast after sunset. He trudged around the corner of the house and entered the bright dome created by the floodlight. It did nothing to warm his ears, which were freezing. However, he didn't want to return inside to get a hat.

The barn was a dark silhouette against the sky, lit by a

sliver of moon the cloud cover threatened to erase from existence.

Barry's pace slowed as he got further from the floodlight. The night absorbed its beams, and Barry descended into darkness. He glanced back at the house, its porch light as dim as a distant star.

Footsteps crunched on the frozen ground, the sound amplified by the wintry evening. Other noises pierced the air—the creak of oak branches in the wind, a huff from a horse in the pen, the *BLZZZ BLZZZ* from the generator box powering the electric fence.

The cold hugged Barry and he shivered. Wanting to bring warmth into his icy fingers, he blew on his hands, which were nearly imperceptible to his eyes. He waved them in front of his face and only saw a slight motion.

His left shoe was loose on his foot, having already come untied. He spent half the day tying that stupid thing.

The barn loomed over him. It stood two stories with a trap door near its peak for ease of loading bales of hay into the loft. The wind caught the unlatched square of plywood and blew it open. It flapped on its hinge before crashing shut again.

BLZZZ BLZZZ from inside the pitch black doorway sent tremors vibrating through Barry's spine.

Playing in this building during the day filled him with joy. Why was it so menacing at night?

Barry braced himself against the doorframe with his right hand. His left reached into the void. A bare lightbulb hung at the far end of the barn—he didn't understand why it wasn't at the entrance. The light's electrical cable wound through the rafters and ended with the three-pronged plug dangling along the wall near the doorway. The ten-year-old groped at it and missed. He tried again and again, reaching higher and leaning further into the structure, to no avail.

Where is it!? Barry felt panic rise through his throat like bile. His arm flailed, and he whacked his wrist on something hard and unseen. He pulled away, clutching his injured appendage. The urge to throw a rock at the barn swelled up inside him, but the night hid the ground from his sight, making it impossible to locate any stones.

He panted, quick and shallow, drawing painful air into his lungs, then shoved the front of his coat up over his mouth and nose to inhale body heat and forced his breathing to slow.

It's okay. You can do this. You can do this. It's just like you've done a million times before.

Two steps forward. Pause. Another step. Pause. One leg stretched out—

CRRRRRKKKKK!

Five quick paces back. His feet slipped and his arms pinwheeled at his side until he caught his balance.

It was the barn settling. Stop being a fraidy cat!

Barry approached the doorway again, the blackness thick inside the building.

Nothing in there that isn't there during the day, he told himself. Except that may not be true. Any sort of animals could have taken shelter—skunks, foxes, bobcats. They could be rabid. Or hungry...eager to taste young human flesh with their sharp teeth...

What if...it's not an animal...

Barry tried to force that idea out of his mind. He was

too old to believe the boogeyman and creatures living under his bed and in his closet. Yet when he went to bed, he insisted the closet door kept shut and the nightlight plugged in, and he tucked his feet under the covers. Just in case.

Monsters were real. Scarier things existed in the world than fantasy creatures. However, his imagination taunted him with visions of what might lurk just out of sight.

BLZZZ BLZZZ

Barry filled his lungs with air, ducked his head, and barged through the doorway like plunging into the deep end of a pool. Blindness engulfed him—not even the beam of the floodlight penetrated this shroud.

His body pivoted, and his hands stretched out, grasping into nothingness.

Any second, something would slither through the endless shadow and grab him from behind…

Barry's palms hit a solid object. The wall. His left hand reached up and landed on the fence's power box. Electricity inside it pulsated.

Was that a wind gust billowing through the barn, or was some creature breathing on his neck?

He clutched at the location the hanging cord should have been. It was not there.

Blood pounded in his temples.

HHHHFFFFF sighed from somewhere behind him.

A scream rose in his throat.

Barry's fingers brushed against a rubbery tendril. He yanked his hand back, convinced he had come in contact with a serpent or a monstrous tentacle.

Wait! The cord!

How could he be so stupid? He thrust his hand into the space where he had touched the cord. Nothing. Then—yes, there it was!

A squeal of relief escaped his dry throat. He licked his chapped lips.

His fingers creeped over the wall, looking for the solitary electrical outlet. Alarm stampeded through his tiny frame as he failed to locate the socket. *It's right there! Why can't I find it?!*

His index finger brushed against the plastic vertical groove, and for a moment, Barry feared he was going to electrocute himself. With a trembling hand, he tried to insert the plug into the outlet. The angle was wrong! Frustration built up in the boy. After an eternity, the plug slid home.

The barn lit up. At the far end of the building, the bulb hanging underneath a rafter like a glowing cyst provided dim illumination. It cast harsh shadows from cobwebs onto the wooden beams and pegboard walls, creating an abstract display of intricate bisecting lines.

Barry exhaled and collapsed against the wall.

BLZZZ BLIZZZ

"Shut up."

The boy plodded through the barn, past waist-high partitions separating sections used as stalls or for storage. Leather saddles, blankets, bridles, and reins hung from pegs on the walls. His eyes fell on an empty hook where the riding crop normally resided. His dad liked to use it on the horses he rode to make them do as he said. He empathized with the animals.

Barry swung open the gate to gain access to old oil

barrels that now contained grain. He pushed the wooden lid off one, which thudded to the sawdust floor. He located a bucket, stepped onto a nearby stool, and leaned into the barrel. Grain filled the metal drum a quarter of the way, so he lowered his entire torso into the cylinder to scoop the grain. With his feet in the air, he teetered on the rim that cut into his stomach. He was glad for his coat's padding. After filling the bucket, he arched his back and flung himself out of the barrel.

Lugging the heavy grain bucket, Barry trudged outside and around to the stalls at the rear. He wondered why his dad kept the animals outside in the elements when there was room inside the barn. Of course, he figured it would've ended up being his job to stable them every night, so he refrained from asking.

The horses waited for him in their individual stalls, knowing it was dinnertime. Gallant was his favorite, a gentle gray gelding Barry rode from time to time when his dad was present. But he considered the brown mare Spartan a doody-head, as it was more than likely to bite or kick. His dad tried to force Spartan to behave and got furious at the horse's behavior, and the riding crop came out often. Barry enjoyed feeding Gallant apples, which the horse ate right out of his hand. For Spartan, he'd toss the fruit to the ground, and if they landed in manure, so be it.

Enough light leaked through cracks in the wall to cast a dim gloom on the horses. Barry hefted the bucket and poured equal amounts of grain into the feeding bins. He scratched Gallant's nose. "There you go, big guy." He ignored Spartan, having learned that lesson.

Barry returned inside the barn, grateful for the shelter

from the stinging wind. He dropped the bucket, then struggled to push the wooden lid over the barrel. Upon sealing the container, he ambled back to the front to unplug the light, his shoe needing to be tied once again.

BLZZZ BLIZZZ

Maybe tomorrow he'd find batteries for the flashlight.

He gripped the plug and pulled. The barn plunged into solid darkness.

Barry headed to the exit.

Something fell on his shoulder. It squeezed.

The boy spun around and inhaled.

Several feet above him, red eyes flared.

Warm breath reeking of decayed meat flowed down on him.

He attempted to scream, but his voice had dried up.

A low rumble emanated from the black emptiness. A deep bass growl.

Hot moisture hit Barry's face. Spittle.

The grip on his shoulder squeezed again. Pain erupted through his arm, spurring him into motion.

Barry wrenched his body away from the claw, spiraled toward the doorway, and bolted. He focused on the floodlight, his beacon.

Frigid wind tore into him as he passed through the door.

Legs pumped. Lungs burned with frosty air.

The claw clamped onto his left ankle, and he toppled face-down on the hard ground. Barry kicked, trying to free his leg from the grasp that now sent searing pain up the appendage.

The top half of the beast leaned out of the barn, its

giant head disproportionate with its sinewy body. Red eyes stared. Mouth opened, revealing yellow fangs and emitting a wheezing growl. *HHHHFFFFF.*

The creature lunged backward, disappearing into the dark emptiness of the building. It yanked on Barry's leg, flipped him onto his back, and dragged him across the frozen ground.

Barry's voice returned—he screamed.

His coat and shirt rode up, exposing his bare back to the rocky terrain that gouged long strips into his skin.

The nightmare holding Barry in its grip raised its other arm, which ended in a lengthy, whip-like tendril. It cracked above the child.

The inky blackness beyond the barn door grew large. In moments, it would swallow him.

His untied shoe popped off.

The claw slid across Barry's sock…and slipped down his small foot and past his toes.

Barry was free.

He scrambled onto his hands and knees, then clamored to his feet—only one of which was shoed. He dashed away with speed he didn't know he had.

The claw whooshed past him, missing him by an inch. It ripped through the hard-packed soil.

Barry ran. And ran and ran.

The floodlight blinded him, but he took no notice.

He burst into the garage. His left foot was cold, so cold, but he didn't care. He barged into the house and raced up the stairs, not hearing his dad yell, "Damn it, what the hell I say about closing that door?!"

The upstairs hallway didn't register to Barry, who

scurried to his room, slammed the door shut, and dove onto his bed. He wriggled under the covers and curled up into a ball.

The bedroom door flew open. The light from the hall silhouetted the large, intimidating shape of his father in the doorway. Barry peered up at him and then at the riding crop the man held.

"You don't listen, boy. There are consequences."

The nightlight reflected in his bloodshot eyes, making them glow red.

Brandon poured gasoline all over the rowboat and doused Mick. His brother looked peaceful, even though his body lay at an awkward angle in the small craft.

"Are you sure about this?" Wes asked. Wide eyes darted nervously, as if expecting a SWAT team to spring out from any direction. However, this was an isolated part of the beach attached to a deserted fish camp surrounded by forest. They stood at the end of the long, narrow dock. The Atlantic stretched into the twilight before them while the sun descended behind the tree line at their backs.

"It's what he wanted." Brandon shook the gas can, flinging the last few drops onto the boat. It was true, Mick made it clear his entire life that he desired a Viking funeral. Every time the subject of death came up—with the brothers, that was often because they shared a love of the macabre—Mick would reiterate his desire for how to dispose of his earthly remains.

"Light it up and put it out to sea," he would say. "Just like the Vikings."

Brandon waggled his fingers to make a "come here" motion. Ginny, an on-again-off-again romantic partner of Mick's since they were in their teens, brought over a wreath on a wire-framed stand. Emblazoned across the front were the words, "HAPPY HOMECOMING!" Their friend Curt, who hung back behind the group as usual, did maintenance for the local school district and snagged it from the trash, the homecoming being a week earlier. Mick would've seen the humor in it.

Ginny handed Brandon the wreath, and he positioned its tripod over Mick's chest so it wouldn't topple into the water. He climbed back onto the dock. "Anyone want to say anything?"

"What the hell," Wes said and glanced over his shoulder to see if the SWAT team had arrived yet. He took a swig of his beer, then looked down at his best friend. "You were such an idiot. I don't know how we managed to stay out of trouble…well, mostly. You never thought you'd live this long. We all figured you'd be murdered by some jealous husband or drive a car off the edge of a canyon or something. Sure didn't expect cancer to get you."

It was a quick illness, fortunately. Mick was always a thin, wiry guy, so his weight loss wasn't dramatic, though it was noticeable. Wes was the one who advised him to get checked out. "You're beginning to look like the Crypt Keeper," he told Mick. News from the doctor was grim— metastatic pancreatic cancer.

The end came within months. He owned few possessions, so putting his affairs in order was a simple task. He owed too much on his house, having only purchased it a year before, so they were going to let it revert to the mortgage company. His car would go to his teenage son Adam, who lived with Mick's ex out of state. Brandon would inherit Mick's extensive science fiction and horror movie and book collection—that was another passion the brothers shared.

At first, Mick felt little pain, but soon agony developed in his stomach and spread through his abdomen and into his back. He self-medicated, because what did he have to lose? That kept him in a state of numbness, both physically and mentally. One night when he was somewhat clear-headed, he told Brandon, "Remember. Viking funeral. I'm counting on you."

"I won't let you down."

Brandon, his parents, and friends checked on Mick often, but ultimately, he died alone in bed. When he didn't answer the phone for two days, Brandon went to Mick's house and found him. Mick's death was expected— regardless, making the call to everyone tore Brandon up. Regardless, he saw it through.

Their mom took it hard. After all, Mick was her firstborn. As she said, children should not die before their parents.

The proper funeral was scheduled for later in the week with Mick's body to be cremated. Cousins and friends from out of town planned to attend. Even Mick's ex, who he affectionately referred to as The Beast, was traveling in with Adam, who would drive Mick's car back home afterward. Brandon knew the ceremony had to happen, mostly for his parents. However, he had a promise to keep to Mick.

He confided in Mick's closest friends—Wes, Ginny,

and Curt—and gave them an option to take part in this foolishness or bow out with no hard feelings. They all agreed.

The fish camp was the obvious choice for the location because the guys spent a lot of weekends up there drinking and fishing and drinking some more. None of them were city boys, but Mick liked the isolation and being surrounded by nature. He occasionally traveled there alone to get away from everything for a few days. He even told Brandon that he'd like to die up there, but his condition worsened, so he was unable to leave his house. Fortunately, they had no trouble booking the fish camp, since it was unoccupied in the middle of the week.

The big issue was how to attain Mick's body. They considered breaking into the funeral home and stealing it, but that would cause many problems, mainly how upsetting it would be to his parents to learn that their son's body was stolen. Ultimately, it was easier than they expected—they bribed a tech who worked at the morgue. Ginny worked with the guy's sister at the warehouse and often hung out with her after their shift ended, so Ginny prodded her for information.

"He likes to be called Frog," Ginny's coworker told her.

"What? Why?"

Her friend shrugged. "What do you expect from someone who willingly works in a morgue?"

Ginny found out the water heater in Frog's house had stopped working and he was unable to afford a new one. Brandon, Ginny, and Curt cornered him after work and made him an offer—they would buy him a new heater and Curt would install it if he let them take Mick's corpse.

Brandon would even throw in an additional thousand dollars as an incentive. They couldn't reveal the truth, so they told him Mick wanted to be buried in a special place in the woods his parents disapprove of. They needed to go through with the ceremony in the funeral home, so they arranged for the ashes from another customer to be divided between that person's and Mick's urns. Nobody would check on the amount of ashes each urn should hold. Frog agreed.

"Guys, how are we going to get him to the fish camp?" Wes asked. "No offense to Mick, but I don't really wanna be driving around with a corpse riding shotgun."

"The morgue has body bags," Curt said. "Could we borrow one?"

Wes scrunched up his face. "What about…you know, the smell?"

Ginny chimed in. "They keep bodies in coolers, so there won't be any odor right away. But if we're going to do the thing at sunset, he'll need to be kept cold. Maybe we can fill the trunk with ice?"

"It'll melt," Brandon said. "And flood my car."

Curt snapped his fingers. "There's a big stand-up cooler at the fish camp. For fish."

"Yeah! He should fit in that," Wes said.

Late that night, the foursome met Frog at the morgue. He had already turned off the security cameras and let them in. The post mortem room was chilly and sterile, with a sweet and sickly odor of embalming chemicals hanging thick in the air. Frog opened one door in the bank of cold storage units and pulled out the table with Mick's prone body lying on it.

"He's naked!" Wes said.

"Well, yeah," Frog said. "You think we dress them for storage?"

"Let's get him into the body bag," Brandon said. He had already arranged for that understanding that they'd return the bag after their ceremony.

Wes, Ginny, and Curt stared at him, not moving.

"What? Think he was gonna walk by himself?"

"I'll help," Frog said. He set the large black bag on a gurney and unzipped it, then he and Brandon took hold of the cadaver and moved it into the open bag. Afterward, Frog zipped it back up.

Brandon scowled at the others. "We gotta put him in the car. I can't do it by myself."

"I've cleaned up enough dead animals in my life," Curt said. "I'll just pretend he's a big dog."

As they carried the body bag to the parking lot, Brandon wished the orange street light right outside the back door wasn't lit. He expected a police cruiser to pass by right then, because that's the way things always worked. However, they slid him into the backseat of the Brandon's car with no mishap.

Brandon drove to the fish camp with Mick in the back while the others rode in Curt's pickup truck, carrying a rowboat they just purchased.

The gravity of what they were doing weighed on Brandon. He owed Mick this. He wasn't often the best brother—he and Mick fought over stupid things, and once the two engaged in a fistfight. Brandon often called him terrible names in fits of anger or frustration. He could be jealous of his older sibling, seeing advantages he had with their parents while Mick often accused him of special treatment because he was the baby of the family. Stupid squabbles that amounted to nothing.

Yet, the good times outweighed the bad. Most days, they were simply brothers, comfortable and content with each other as an ordinary family. Brandon never realized how extraordinary that was.

He was the more studious of the two, whereas Mick barely graduated because of his lack of interest in school. After a stint in the military, Mick settled for a career of manual labor while Brandon pursued a college education and then got an accounting position with a mid-level corporation. Mick teased him about his boring desk job, but on rare occasions said he was proud of his little brother for doing good with his life—something Mick seemed unable to do. Brandon consoled him during Mick's breakup with The Beast as well as for every other of the dozen breakups Mick had thereafter. Brandon once told him, "You suck at relationships, but I admire your perseverance."

More importantly, Mick was there for Brandon. He was the big brother who he went to for advice on sex when he was sixteen and wanted desperately to lose his virginity, and who he bragged to when it finally happened at age twenty. Mick was with him the first time Brandon got drunk and helped hide the fact from their parents. Mick counseled him through every crisis of his life and encouraged him when things became overwhelming. They led very different lives, but Brandon knew he could count on Mick when it mattered.

And now he was gone.

Well, not totally—he was in the backseat awaiting his final voyage.

They arrived at the fish camp, which was musty and dusty. It was the off-season, so it didn't show much use recently. The large wooden cabin had a main open sitting room with old furniture, a basic kitchen, several bedrooms containing rickety beds, and a back area for cleaning fish. There, Wes located the top-loading chest cooler, plugged it in, and removed the empty shelves. Brandon and Curt carried the body bag from the car and awkwardly fit it into the appliance by bending the bag at odd angles.

"Doesn't look too comfortable," Wes said.

That night, they got drunk and shared stories about Mick, laughing and crying until nearly three a.m. It was what Mick would've wanted. He wasn't one for ceremony —except for the Viking tradition—and preferred people to enjoy themselves rather than wallow in misery. Sharing the memories helped deal with the pain.

They slept most of the morning. When they awoke, they remained quiet and kept to themselves. Brandon spent the morning hiking the trails in the woods. While he joined his brother here occasionally, this was really Mick's place of respite. He understood why Mick liked it so much, as the forest and the rocky shoreline were beautiful. It felt a million miles from civilization.

The afternoon crept along until it was time to make preparations. Brandon had Curt help him remove Mick from the freezer and brought the body bag into one bedroom and on a bed. When Brandon was alone, he unzipped the bag and looked down at Mick's remains. It was like a wax dummy of a celebrity—identical features, but in a surreal, uncanny valley way. It hit Brandon that Mick was truly finished with this world, and he was looking at an empty container. It didn't matter if this thing was buried, cremated, or swallowed by the ocean because it wasn't really his brother. Just an object that used to carry life.

Brandon dressed the body in clothes Mick loved to wear—black jeans, a Def Leppard T-shirt, leather hiking boots, and a camo jacket. He also combed Mick's hair. Brandon considered shaving him, but Mick usually went around with several day's growth of beard anyway, so leaving him unshaven seemed more respectful.

He felt the gaze of his companions on him as he stepped out of the bedroom. "All right. Let's do this."

Curt located a wheelbarrow and rolled it to the back door.

"Seriously?" Wes asked.

"I ain't gonna carry him all the way down to the dock," Curt said.

Brandon and Curt placed Mick in the wheelbarrow, then crossed his arms over his chest. Curt pushed the cart. Halfway down the hill to the rocky shoreline, one of Mick's hands flopped over and dangled, fingers nearly touching the dirt. Brandon put it back in place.

The guys had already secured the rowboat to the end of the dock, so Brandon and Curt carried Mick to it.

"Don't drop him in the water," Ginny said.

"How are we gonna do this?" Brandon asked. The rope connecting the rowboat to the dock allowed the boat to drift a couple of feet away.

"You get in," Curt said. "I'll lower him down to you."

Brandon climbed down into the vessel and nearly toppled over when he lost his balance, but grabbed the dock before he plunged into the water.

Curt moved Mick into a sitting position with his legs hanging over the planks. "Wes, help me."

"I ain't touching him."

"Get over here!"

Wes didn't budge.

"Oh for—move." Ginny pushed Wes aside. He stumbled and almost went into the drink himself.

Ginny sat on one side of Mick and assisted as Curt, with his arms under Mick's armpits, lowered the corpse to Brandon in the rowboat. The boat threatened to capsize, but they deposited the body in it. Curt reached out a hand to Brandon and helped him back onto the dock.

Wes gave Brandon the gas can.

After Brandon spread gasoline onto Mick and the boat, he and his friends took turns saying a few words. Even Curt mustered, "I'm gonna miss you, old buddy."

Ginny popped open a bottle of Mick's favorite brand of rum and poured drinks all around. They raised their glasses to Mick and drank.

"You got the torch?" Brandon asked.

"Right here." Curt handed him a broom pole with a swab of cloth tied at one end. He had prepped it by dunking it in the gas can until the material was soaked.

"Untie the boat first," Ginny said. "You don't want that thing going up in flames close to the dock."

Brandon handed her the torch and untied the boat.

"Here." He gave Wes the rope to prevent the rowboat from drifting away.

Curt lit a stick match and touched the tip to the swaddle on the end of the torch. It burst into flames.

"Push it out and I'll throw the torch," Brandon said. Wes tossed the end of the rope into the rowboat and used his feet to launch it from the dock. At first, the tide pushed against it, preventing it from moving out, but finally it began drifting further from the mainland. Brandon flung the lit torch, and it landed squarely on Mick's chest. Flames spread instantly.

Black smoke plumed into the air. Stench of smoldering flesh assaulted them, even from a distance. The others covered their noses with their shirts, but Brandon ignored it. He stood at the end of the dock like a sentinel standing guard while salty sea spray misted onto his face, mixing with his tears. The burning boat took his brother out to the ocean, where it would burn up and deliver Mick's remains to his watery ultimate resting place.

The Vikings would be proud.

Seventy-nine-year-old Abigail Henson peered out at the sunrise over the Atlantic as she sipped a cup of hot tea like she had done most of her adult life. She bought this seaside home after marrying her beloved Henry, twelve years gone. Her existence was comfortable, even while dealing with the aches and pains advanced age brought her.

Something caught her eye. An object had washed up

on the little beach on her property. It looked like burned wood, but was substantial, maybe several feet long.

Making her way outside, Abigail strode across the wooden back porch that seriously needed painting and down the stone walkway through her backyard. As she approached the rocky outcropping, the object revealed itself to be a rowboat—one that was severely charred but had not completely incinerated. She wondered what on earth could've happened to it?

She reached the scorched vessel and gazed down into it. And saw what it carried.

The neighbors heard her shriek.

Mick would have been amused.

This book is dedicated to my older brother, Kenneth Wise, Jr., who passed away unexpectedly right around the New Year of 2024. I spoke about him in the Preface of *Portals of the Mind*, but need to acknowledge him again for the influence he had on shaping my interests in storytelling. He was ten years older than me and we didn't interact a whole lot, though our paths did intertwine through the years. About a decade ago, when I was in need, he sent me a check out of the blue to help me get through my troubles, and the only thing he asked in return was for me to write. I'm honoring that request to the best of my ability. The story "Viking Funeral" included in this volume was inspired by his desire to have one upon his death. Instead, he had a simple military ceremony, which I watched live streamed.

I need to thank several people who helped me develop these stories by providing feedback, advice, and a lot of patience with me: Frank Accardo, Terri Donawell, Eric Kaplan, and Diane Savickas. And, of course, my mom,

Janice Robinson, who has been urging me to focus on my writing. I'm trying, Mom!

Additionally, special thanks needs to go to David Gerrold and the members of The Writer Stuff class who have offered support. David's mentorship has guided me in improving my craft. Any writing errors I may have made are entirely on me and not him.

I also need to give a shoutout to Mike Ensley and the staff and volunteers of Pensacon. My service to the con opened doors that I would never have had access to, and gave me the opportunity to pursue different directions in my career.

At the beginning of this book, I quoted Rod Serling, and of course the title of the book is taken from the opening narration to *The Twilight Zone*. That show and Serling's talent had a huge influence on me. While it's known for its twist endings (which I love), the heart of the show is its humanity and how it explores social issues.

One thing that *TZ* did often was show horrible characters get their comeuppance, usually in fantastical ways. That was the inspiration for "A Perfect Copy", an absurdist take on that theme. Hey, if Stephen King can write about a killer laundry machine, I can do one about a copier. What's notable about this story, however, is that it's the first one I ever had published. It appeared in *Absolute Literary Journal* in the spring of 1988 (in a slightly different form), published by Oklahoma City Community College, where I had been attending to earn my A.A. in broadcasting.

The only other "trunk story" that I dusted off was "Closing Time". Unfortunately, the surrealism of this tale may be too close to reality these days. The rest of the stories in this collection are new.

If you enjoyed this book, do me a solid and leave a review on various platforms where it's sold. Doing so assists the all-powerful algorithm in finding the book homes with new readers. Follow me on social media and see what kinds of useless stuff I post.

Until next time…

About the Author

Stephen Wise is a multiple award-winning screenwriter and filmmaker with a Bachelor's degree in film production from the University of Central Florida. His films have been screened in over a dozen countries. He is the co-writer of *Batman: DarKnight,* which IFC hailed as one of the seven best unproduced Batman screenplays. He is a Michigan native and currently resides in Northwest Florida.

To find out more about Stephen Wise and his work, visit StephenJWise.com

amazon.com/stores/Stephen-Wise/author/B00R25T4YY

facebook.com/stephenwisefilmmaker

threads.net/@stephenjwise

linkedin.com/in/stephenjwise

instagram.com/stephenwiseauthor

bsky.app/profile/stephenjwise.bsky.social

goodreads.com/stephenwise

Arrowhead Publications

If you enjoyed this book, be sure to write a review of it on your favorite platform to help other people discover it.

To learn more about Arrowhead Publications and its books, visit arrowheadpublications.com or scan the QR code to go to the website.

Follow us on social media.

facebook.com/arrowheadpublications
instagram.com/arrowheadpublications
threads.net/@arrowheadpublications
bsky.app/profile/arrowheadpubs.bsky.social